# Harvest of the Witch

A Paranormal Women's Fiction Mystery

## Kirsten Weiss

misterio press

# About this Book

**H**alloween is coming... And so is murder...

Doyle witch Karin has it all. A loving husband. Two wonderful children. A flexible career. Now that her days of fighting dark magicians is over, she's perfectly happy in her comfortable life. But beneath the surface of perfection, cracks are beginning to emerge.

So when a witch she's mentoring asks for help, Karin might be a little too eager to escape her routine. Until she arrives at the remote mansion retreat to find her apprentice is dead.

Exploring the fragile balance between love and longing, happiness and deception, Karin must follow the trail of dark magic to its end. But can she overcome not only a killer, but her own inner demons?

A thrilling supernatural mystery, packed with Halloween magic and murder! It's perfect for fans of paranormal women's fiction. This short read is book 11 in the Witches of Doyle mystery series and a prequel to Kirsten Weiss's new Mystery School series.

# Introducing the UnTarot App: Step into the Enchantment of Kirsten Weiss's Mystery School Series!

E mbark on a journey that intertwines fiction and reality as you dive into the captivating world of Kirsten Weiss's upcoming Mystery School series. With the UnTarot app, you can wield the very cards the characters from the books utilize, tapping into a wellspring of ancient wisdom and boundless magic.

Imagine harnessing the power of the Un Tarot cards to unlock hidden insights and unravel the threads of fate. With the Un Tarot app, you gain access to a treasure trove of captivating readings and interpretations. As you explore this mystical experience, you'll be drawn into a world where the boundaries between fiction and reality blur.

- **Authentic Connection:** Immerse yourself in the enchanting ambiance of the Mystery School series. The Un Tarot app faithfully captures the essence of the books, allowing you to connect with the characters and their adventures on a whole new level.

- **Ancient Wisdom, Modern Convenience:** The Un Tarot app marries centuries-old divination techniques with cutting-edge technology, creating an accessible experience for both seasoned practitioners and curious novices.

- **Free Exploration**: Yes, you read that right! The Un Tarot app is entirely FREE, ensuring that everyone can join in the magical journey of self-discovery, insight, and revelation.

Ready to embark on a journey that defies the boundaries of time and space? The Un Tarot app beckons you to step into the wondrous world of Kirsten Weiss's Mystery School series. Download the Un Tarot app and let the magic unfold before your very eyes!

# Download the UnTarot app for FREE today and embrace the enchantment that awaits!

# Copyright

Book Cover by Dar Albert

Illustrations licensed via DepositPhotos.com

misterio press / March, 2023

Visit the author website to sign up for updates on upcoming books and fun, free stuff: KirstenWeiss.com

# Contents

LISTEN

# Chapter 1

I t was a mansion worthy of the season. Maple trees, blazing gold and persimmon, dotted the wide lawn. Pumpkins promenaded up the stone steps to a door beneath a gothic arch. The October sun glinted against tall, lead-paned windows.

If the place was haunted, it was a cheerful haunting, the sort that would welcome costumed children. Not that there would be any of those within walking distance. The point of an estate like this was elite isolation.

My phone on speaker, I stepped from my SUV onto the gravel drive. My young daughter babbled from the phone's speaker.

The afternoon was hot, as California autumns could sometimes be. But a winter shiver rippled my spine. Suddenly, I was afraid.

I hadn't been afraid when I'd made the decision to come. I'd been determined and a little excited. My sister Jayce couldn't leave her coffee shop. Lenore couldn't abandon her bookstore. It was on me, the work-from-home witch, and Nick and I had agreed I needed a break.

I shifted my weight on the gravel. After all, it had only been a suspicion of Sunny's, and she was still a new witch. There was nothing here that screamed of dark magic.

Since my phone was in hand and Emmie's chatter on full flow, I tapped our mystery school's UnTarot app. A picture appeared on the screen, with one word beneath it: *Listen*.

Well, I'd be listening all right. And watching and using every witchy sense I had to confirm or deny Sunny's suspicion.

I relaxed my gaze. Three shoulder-height lines of energy brightened the air.

Remembering Emmie on the phone, I bit back my curse. The red earth energy—ley lines—intersected somewhere inside the gray-stone mansion. Their combined power created a reddish aura around the house as if it were lit by demonic energy.

But ley lines weren't evil. They were just power. Neutral. Ancient societies had built sacred structures and cities atop them, marking their connecting points. And the ley lines had imbued those structures with power.

This mansion had certainly benefited from the ley lines. It had magic in spades. Sunny had been right about that at least.

My shoulders curled forward, my stomach heavying. I hoped Sunny was wrong about the rest.

Other human-sized energetic cords appeared at the edges of the ley lines' red corona, which was so bright it seemed to absorb the smaller cords' energy. But I could still see that one of the smaller ones was dark and cruel and cold.

I swallowed. So Sunny was right about that too. Like me, she was able to see the energies connecting people and things. Most of those ties were unconscious attachments—the love for a family member, the anger toward a colleague.

But the conscious attachments, the spells, were always dark. Spells to control. Spells to manipulate. Spells to harm.

Shaking myself, I grabbed my professional-grade backpack from the car and slung the blue bag over one shoulder. I turned the phone off speaker and clapped it to my ear.

My son Mitch's voice rose in a shriek above Emmie's chatter. Wincing, I jerked the phone away, made a soothing noise, and strode toward the wide stone steps.

"I have to go, Emmie. Put your dad on the phone."

Instead, my daughter loosed a last flood of childish intel. A blue bird at the window. A boy being mean. A red jacket. Somehow, these were all connected in pre-kindergarten land, though I had no idea how.

"How *interesting*," I said. "Now put your father on. I have to go to work."

I climbed the wide steps and rang the bell. I half expected an ominous gong in response. But the house was too well-mannered to permit sound to escape.

I craned my neck and studied the paned windows above. A house this size would need a staff. Would there be a butler? I imagined a cadaverous man in a tux. A bug-eyed hunchback. A toothy male model.

The arched wooden door opened. A little old woman in a jungle-print kimono, jeans, and a white tee blinked at me. Her ivory hair was piled high on her head.

Abruptly, she moved forward as if to grasp my hand. The fabric of her kimono caught on the doorknob, jerking her arm back. "Oh!" She untangled herself. "You must be Karin."

"Sorry." I motioned to the phone at my ear. "My daughter won't... She's four."

The woman pressed her wrinkled hands together. "Such a precious age." She drew a long breath, her pale blue eyes somber. "But the thing is, I have bad news."

My stomach plunged. The job had been canceled. I knew it had been a stretch for Sunny to bring me in as a consulting "word witch." The title itself was outrageous, even if I did have several dozen romance novels under my belt.

Emmie was still talking, oblivious, and I realized it didn't matter if I listened or not. My responses wouldn't alter her flow. I lowered the phone. "Bad news?"

So Sunny's boss had decided against me. That was fine. I didn't need to get inside. Those lines had told me enough. What I needed now was to get Sunny *out*.

"It's Sunny, you see." The woman tugged at the gold medallion around her neck. "I'm afraid..." She drew herself up. "I'm sorry, there's no good way to say this. She's dead."

My breath huffed as if I'd been gut punched. Something clattered to the paving stones. "What?" I couldn't move, couldn't speak, couldn't inhale. It couldn't be real. It was a joke. Sunny wasn't dead. She'd emailed me yesterday.

Her gnarled fingers hadn't released the medallion—a primitive sun. She gripped it as if it were a talisman for a cruel and pagan god, one that had sapped the life from her. The woman's skin looked fragile and papery. There was vulnerability in her eyes, and shock, and pain.

She wasn't joking.

The woman released the medallion, and it fell, gleaming, to her chest. Swiftly, she stooped and retrieved the phone I'd dropped. "I shouldn't have said it like that. I should have warned you to prepare yourself. I'm so sorry." She extended the phone toward me.

As if my hand was being lifted by someone else, I took it. "When? How?" I croaked, my neck cording.

I hadn't known Sunny well. But I'd *known* her. Sunny had been a part of our school. A student. A woman like me, one who could see more than she should.

"This morning. It was a terrible accident. She must have slipped and hit her head. We found her in the pool." Her pale eyes widened. "You look like you're about to faint. Come inside." The woman grasped my arm.

I winced at the strength of her near-supernatural grip. She led me, un-resisting, into the mansion.

I had the vague impression of teeth and snarling animals, and then the weight of past lives. When I shook off my fugue state, I found myself in a sitting room. It smelled of flowers and furniture polish. Bookshelves lined its dark wood walls.

But instead of the leather-bound classics I'd have expected in a grand room like this, their shelves were lined with well-loved spines. Paperback romances. Agatha Christies. An old yellow set of Nancy Drews.

"She was really looking forward to your arrival." The woman sat on a green leather sofa. "Again, I'm so sorry for your loss."

My jaw tightened. "Sorry, who are you?" I asked, my voice a blade.

Sunny was dead. *Dead*. And I was suddenly furious at this strange woman. Who the hell was she, waltzing around in a kimono and jeans and dropping death news like it was no big thing? *About Sunny.*

I tried to quiet my breathing. Sunny'd only been... what? Not quite thirty. She'd just broken up with her boyfriend when we'd met, and I'd felt... sympathy and a certain smug comfort at my own settled, marital state.

The feeling had flushed me with shame then. The memory felt worse now.

Lowering myself into a matching wingchair, I glanced down at my phone. It hadn't broken, but I'd somehow disconnected, probably when I'd dropped it.

She made an embarrassed moue. "Please forgive me. I didn't introduce myself. I'm Georgette. Georgette Winsome."

I felt the blood drain from her face. "You're..."

Georgette's smile was faint. "Just Georgette. Just a normal woman, my dear. And I'm still reeling too."

Georgette Winsome was *not* a normal woman. Not by a longshot. She had more money than Bill Gates and used it to better purpose. She'd been married to the shipping magnate Frank Winsome—an unhappy marriage by all accounts.

Frank had died in a boating accident forty years ago. Georgette had been playing the merry widow ever since.

"Can I get you some tea?" she asked. "Or something stronger?"

I hesitated. *Oh, what the hell?* "Something stronger."

Georgette rose and walked to a liquor trolly. "Brandy? Vodka? Whiskey?"

"Vodka," I said. "With ice."

"Vodka *is* best cold," she agreed, returning with a tinkling glass.

I held it a long moment, feeling the chill of the tumbler on my fingers, the sharpness of the cut glass pressing into my skin. Then I slugged back the drink and grimaced at the shock of alcohol. "What happened?"

"A stupid slip and fall." Georgette sat again, her kimono billowing around her rounded hips. "Sunny was in the habit of taking a morning swim. She was an early riser, up by five-thirty, I think she told us. Berkeley found her."

Avoiding her gaze, I found a white-stone coaster and set the glass on it. "Berkeley?" I asked, feigning ignorance. Sunny had already filled me in on the suspects.

"My nephew. Bob helped pull her from the pool, but by then it was too late. She was gone. Bob tried. He pumped so much water from her lungs, but..." Her mouth trembled.

"Bob?"

"Bob Wodge, the artist. He's been barricaded in his studio, painting, ever since. I think he had a crush on Sunny. Such a waste," she said, her voice mournful. "I can't believe she's gone. She was so *young*, your age, I think."

I studied the Persian carpet between my tennis shoes. I was a little older than Sunny. She would never reach my age now. Nausea spun inside my stomach. "Where... Where is she?"

"The ambulance took her away. There will be an autopsy. I told them to make it a priority."

And they would. My muscles stiffened. Georgette Winsome generally got what she wanted, when she wanted.

"She said she had a foster brother," Georgette said quietly.

I shook my head. Sunny hadn't spoken much of her past, but I knew she'd been raised in foster care. My nails bit into my palms. The system hadn't been kind to her.

The system hadn't been kind, but Sunny had risen above it, made something of the bad deal she'd been handed. And now she was dead.

"She spoke highly of you," the older woman continued.

My throat tightened. I knew why Sunny had said those things—not because of any great admiration for me, but to get me inside the house. That knowledge was no comfort. I'd come too late.

"What can I do to help you?" Georgette asked. "You've come all the way from Doyle, I think?"

"Yes." But I couldn't return. Not yet. Not with Sunny's job unfinished. I didn't see how I could stay here though. "I should... get a hotel. It's too far to drive back tonight."

"Nonsense," Georgette said. "I mean, if that's what you want, of course I'll take care of it. But you can stay here. I've got plenty of room, and it's the least I can do."

Some of the tension leaked from my shoulders. "That... Yes, thank you. If it's not too much trouble," I added insincerely.

Hugging her sleeves close to avoid the knobs at the end of the bannisters, she led me up a magnificent curving set of stairs. I followed her down a long hallway to a room fit for an Italian countess. Antique jungle-print wallpaper, a ceiling decorated with golden curlicues, a canopy bed with pink velvet drapes.

"Sunny thought you'd like it," Georgette said quietly.

I nodded, finding it hard again to speak. "Thank you," I managed.

"I'll leave you to... Well. There's no password on the guest internet. There's also no formal dinnertime, and you don't have to join us if you'd prefer privacy. But we usually find ourselves around the dining table at six."

"I'll be there," I said.

Georgette nodded and backed from the room. She closed the door behind her.

I dropped my pack on the bed and wandered to the glass patio doors. Mt. Shasta, wreathed in clouds, loomed in the distance. Then I returned to the bed, extracted my laptop from my pack, and opened it on the antique desk.

Sunny had wanted me here.

And Georgette had killed her.

❖❖ ⋯ ✦ ⋯ ❖❖

SUBJECT: Black Lodge

Karin:

I'm not sure if I have black lodges on the brain after the story you told me about that gang of dark magicians. But I saw a symbol that looked a lot like the one you showed me. I only saw it for an instant, but it was enough to make me try and *see*. And I saw a cord a lot like the one you described, dark and dripping. It's hooked into someone I *like*—Mrs. Winsome. Yes, *that* Winsome, Georgette Winsome. She's brought me to her home to lead a private awareness and meditation retreat, and I feel like I'm in over my head.

I've asked her if she'd be interested in having you come as well to lead a creative journaling practice. I've told her you're a word witch. If you can't come, I get it. I know this is out of the blue. But If I'm wrong, this place is like a spa. And if I'm right... I'd really rather not be right. But there's something *wrong* here.

Can you come and just take a look? Let me know if I'm going out of my mind?

- Sunny

# Chapter 2

It's hard to stay suspicious when drinking good wine. So I reluctantly turned down what no doubt would have been the finest Burgundy to pass my lips.

I focused on the steak. It was the best and most tender I'd ever eaten. I had a tough time choking it down.

The dining room rivaled Camelot's. It was no doubt more comfortable than that fabled castle. Flowers spilled from centerpieces. Chandeliers sparkled above the long table. A fire crackled in the stone fireplace, heating the tall back of my chair.

We'd clustered at the table's end by the picture windows, reflecting ebony in the night. Our silence was thick, heavy, and awkward— broken only by the sound of cutlery on china plates, glasses being returned to the wooden table, a cough.

I relaxed my gaze and turned my head toward Georgette. A dark cord extended from her chest and across the table. My pulse stumbled. So she *was* the puppet master. But who were her puppets?

Widening my vision to take in the others, I froze. Dark cords connected them all.

Panicked, I glanced down at my own chest. But it was clear, the only attachments the heart energy of my ties to the people I loved. Uncertainly, I relaxed.

I ran my free hand down the thighs of my forest-green slacks. Georgette was still the most likely villain. But in this knot of spells, it was impossible to be certain who had created the dark attachments, and who were the victims.

Georgette cleared her throat. "Karin, tell me about your journaling practice. How does it work?"

I started. *Right.* I was supposed to be a magical journaling coach. "Ah. Yes."

I cleared my throat and scrambled for the patter I'd practiced on the drive here. "We all have stories we tell ourselves. Sometimes they're helpful. Sometimes they're not."

*What story do you tell yourself? How do you rationalize* your *crimes?*

"I imagine our stories are rarely accurate," Georgette said with a small smile.

"No," I said shortly. And the truth mattered. But it could be hard to get at. "The goal of this type of journaling is to explore our inner landscapes and rewrite the stories we tell ourselves, so we can become the people we want to be."

The words sounded as stiff and false as they were. *A word witch. What a joke.*

Bob Wodge, the artist, grunted. He was a big man with faded reddish hair and a leathery tan. "Never was much of a writer. Prefer the visual arts." He shoved a piece of steak into his mouth.

"Well," Georgette said fondly, "you would, wouldn't you? But Bob wouldn't need to actually *write*, would he? Not with all those modern dictation programs." She looked to me.

"Dictation would work," I said quickly. "Just getting your thoughts down is powerful. I was doing some journaling myself earlier, about Sunny."

Georgette reached across the table and clasped my hand. It was all I could do not to jerk away from her touch.

"I'm so sorry," she said. "I keep saying it, and those words feel inadequate. *Sorry for your loss.* We say it because we can't think of anything else, but they don't convey anything of meaning, do they? I've been wandering around, feeling hollow and wondering…"

Georgette blinked rapidly. She turned her ivory head toward the picture windows overlooking the dark swell of lawn.

"It wasn't your fault." Her nephew, Berkeley, glared at me. He was tall and blond and chiseled like a Greek statue, and he looked a bit younger than me.

"But we can't say that," she said. "Not for sure. The pavement around the pool was slick—"

"Because it's a *pool*," Berkeley said. "And there are warning signs, and she swam regularly. Though it's ridiculous that you even have a heated pool. All this house for one person is a waste."

"But the house isn't for just one person," Georgette said blandly. "There's you and Bob and Matt and Su—" She bit her bottom lip. An uncomfortable silence fell.

"Maybe it *was* my fault." Georgette blinked rapidly.

"Sunny knew the risks," Berkeley said.

"But do we really know the risks?" the third man at the table asked in a low tone. Matt Power was slight and dark, with the long, narrow hands of a musician, which he was. "We tell ourselves we know what we're facing, but we don't want to really look at it, at our future deaths."

The artist snorted. "*I* know," he said, chewing. "I talk to the dead on the daily."

Berkeley rolled his eyes. "Ah, yes. Your supernatural *art*."

"Karin's an artist too," Georgette said. "She made a Tarot deck." She turned to me. "Sunny showed me some of the cards."

My hand twitched, the fork pinging against the plate. "I can't take credit. My sister designed the deck."

And my freewheeling witchy sister, Jayce, had added symbols without understanding why. It had been left to me to interpret the cards and write their explanations. Though in fairness to my sister, the symbols she'd spontaneously chosen all had powerful, cohesive meanings. She was uncanny that way.

"But it's not a Tarot deck," I continued, "not exactly. There's only one suit and fewer cards, so we call it an UnTarot."

"How did your sister make them?" Georgette asked.

*None of your damn business.* "Digital collage."

"That's not art," Bob said.

I stiffened. I tended to agree, but he didn't need to be a jerk about it. And the point of the deck was the symbols and the self-development, not the cards' artistic merit.

"They're beautiful though," Georgette said.

"And what are you working on?" I asked Matt.

"A symphony based on the music of the spheres." He shoved a piece of broccoli to the other side of his plate.

I set down my fork. "The music of the spheres?"

"The sidereal periods of rotation of the planets can be converted into sound frequencies," he said. "We can measure the pitch of every planet in our solar system. Venus is A, Mars is D, Mercury C sharp, creating a pentatonic sequence known as the Kumayoshi mode."

"Fascinating," I murmured, adjusting the white cloth napkin in my lap. I'd taken piano lessons as a child, had hated it, and now could barely read music.

"Would you stay?" Georgette asked me abruptly. "I know it's asking a lot. But I, for one... I think your journaling exercises would help me process what happened today and... other things."

Something inside my chest fluttered, and I set my jaw. "Yes, of course." If I was going to prove she killed Sunny, I'd need to stay.

I just hoped the evidence I gathered would be something I could take to the police. If the only evidence I found was magical, I was sunk.

"What about your staff?" I asked. "Would they like to participate?" They might have seen something, might know something.

Georgette pressed her hands into the white tablecloth. "That's an excellent idea. I'm sure they'd appreciate it as well—a way to process what's happened—though none were here when..." She bit her bottom lip.

"When Sunny died?" I prompted.

"They go home at night and return at eight in the morning," she said. "I never liked the idea of live-in servants. I never liked the idea of servants, actually. But I like the idea of housecleaning this big place on my own even less."

My lips compressed. Yes, a dark magician *would* like her privacy, especially at night. "And Sunny died before eight AM?" I asked. "How can you be sure?"

"I found her around seven," Berkeley said, gruff. Light from the chandelier glinted off his blond head. His jade eyes were shadowed caverns, his cheeks hollow. "She was in her bathing suit."

"And she didn't swim at night," Georgette said, "not after dinner. Cramps, you know. She was very careful."

"Not that careful," her nephew said sharply.

"Oh, Berkeley," she said. "Stop trying to protect me. A woman died in my pool. Of course I've got some responsibility. It was *my pool*."

"You're too—" He bit the word off, his mouth clamping shut.

We finished dinner. Georgette had to cajole, browbeat, and wheedle the men into private journaling sessions with me the next day. With shows of reluctance, they agreed.

She promised to ask her staff if they were interested, and I half hoped, half dreaded they would be. It didn't sound like they could have been witnesses, and certainly not suspects. But they still might have useful information.

Stuffed, I returned to my bedroom and phoned my husband, Nick.

"Karin, how's it going?" he asked, the sound of his voice warming me.

I scrubbed a hand over my face. "Not good." Dropping onto the canopy bed, I told him about Sunny. It was a relief to confide my fears, my guilt. He was my best friend, and he understood.

"An accident?" he asked after a long silence.

"It couldn't have been, could it?" I clawed a hand through my auburn hair. "I mean, what are the odds? And there *is* black lodge activity here."

"The same lodge we encountered before?"

"I can't tell. Sunny thought she'd seen the Brotherhood's symbol somewhere, and the energy *feels* the same." I ran my free hand down a length of velvet bed curtain. "But it's not like any of us have that much experience."

"I'm driving up to Shasta."

My pulse jumped in my throat. "No," I said quickly. If something happened to me... I didn't want it to happen to him too. It wasn't that I was trying to protect Nick—he'd hate that. But Mitch and Emmie needed at least one parent.

And I hated that I had to think about things like that. But too much was at stake. If this was the same black lodge we'd encountered before...

They'd been powerful enough to cast a spell on our small town. It had turned neighbor against neighbor, infected us with panic and suspicion. There'd even been a riot on Main Street. And a murder.

"You need backup," Nick said.

I squeezed my eyes shut. And I wanted backup. I ached with wanting him here. "Yes, but not yet." I flopped back onto the pillows. "They think I'm a journaling coach. I'll do my thing tomorrow, learn what I can, and leave."

"You'll leave tomorrow?"

I'd originally given myself two days, expecting to drive back Halloween morning. But that had assumed I'd be working with Sunny. With her gone...

"I'll be home tomorrow. That will give me more time to prep for the Halloween madness. Consider this a scouting expedition. I won't stick around for more."

Reaching behind my head, I slid my hand beneath the pillow and touched stiff paper. Frowning, I drew out an oversized card. My breath caught.

"What about tonight?" he asked. "Is your room secure?"

*What the hell?* I studied the card then glanced around the room. "Yes," I said vaguely.

"Good. Stay in for the night, will you?"

My heart thumped, roaring in my ears. Incredulous, I returned my focus to the card, a picture of a lighthouse on a rocky cliff in a storm. "Um... Nick, I need to go."

"Is something wrong?"

"No. I'm fine. Tomorrow I'll do the journal thing, and I'll leave. It's.. I've just found one of our UnTarot cards."

"A card from your school? How did it get there? Was it Sunny's?"

"No." It wasn't Sunny's. It wasn't anyone's.

It was definitely one of our UnTarot cards, given to our students to help them progress in magic. And I'd never seen it before.

◆》 ⋯ ◆ ⋯ 《◆

THE LIGHTHOUSE

# Chapter 3

"Well, it's *not* one of ours," my sister Jayce said stubbornly. "I never made a lighthouse card."

I shifted on the canopy bed, one ankle tucked beneath me. The pink and green velvet rippled, as if from a breeze, but the glass patio door was shut.

"But it *is*," I said. "The back is identical. The front... Hold on." I snapped a picture of the front and back of the card with my phone and texted it to her. There was a faint ping on the other end of the line, then a long pause.

"Damn," Jayce said. "It *does* look like one of ours. But it's not. Could Sunny have made it herself?"

"If she did, how did it get under my pillow?" I glanced uneasily at the closed bedroom door. Had Georgette put it here? She'd said she'd seen Sunny's cards. What had happened to them? "You stopped at twenty-five cards, didn't you?"

"Of course I did," she said. "Five times five."

The number of wisdom gained through experience—the ideal number for a mystery school. Also, our printer gave us a deal if we had a max of 25 per pack.

"You don't think..." Jayce hesitated. "Could it be the same black lodge, the Brotherhood?"

The lodge that had tried to gain a foothold in Doyle, to use our small town's magic for its own dark purposes. We still weren't entirely sure what those purposes were.

But actions spoke louder than words, and the actions of the lodge had been murderous. I rubbed the red crescent on the heel of my palm—an old spider bite.

"I checked the card's energies. It's not black lodge." I relaxed my gaze again. There was a faint, gold and pink halo around the card, and no ties leading to or from it.

And there *should* have been connecting lines. *Someone* had made the card, and they'd used magic. The energies of the maker should be imprinted on it. "It's like..." I rubbed my forehead.

But it couldn't be an apport, a material object sent from the spirit world. The card had the same paper and coating from the print shop we'd found online. It wasn't made of ectoplasm. That substance had a different feel.

"Like what?" Jayce prompted.

"It's got energy, but there are no energetic ties. It's like... Well, it's like an apport, but I'd swear the material it's made of isn't ectoplasm. The card even has the same *feel* as ours." Premium smooth coating. Three-hundred gsm weight.

"Sunny must have made it," Jayce said firmly. "There's no other explanation."

I tossed the card to the pink and cream coverlet. "Maybe."

"Are you sure it's not black lodge? The imagery's a little... dark."

"But it isn't. A lighthouse is a sign of hope, of guidance, of lighting the way. It's like the Hermit card in Tarot, alone on a mountaintop, a journey of self-discovery that lights the way for others."

"A journey?" Jayce asked, tone dubious. "Lighthouses don't journey."

My mouth puckered. Jayce knew symbols were rarely literal. "Okay, maybe not a journey, but everything else I said tracks."

"Sunny. I can't believe this." Jayce sighed. "Aside from the card, did you learn anything?"

I told her about what I'd found so far. "I'm not seeing something where it's not, am I? Her death *could* have been an accident."

Jayce's laugh was hollow. "You said you saw black-lodge energy. What are the odds her death was natural?"

*Near to zero.* My shoulders dropped. "I liked Sunny," I said quietly. And I had a sick feeling we'd failed her.

"Everyone liked Sunny," Jayce said. "She was just like her name. When you get home... We'll figure this out."

"I know." It hadn't been arrogance that had led us to start the mystery school. It had been hope. We'd survived multiple trials by fire, and we hoped we could help others. I had to keep believing. "I'll see you tomorrow."

We said our goodbyes and disconnected. I studied the card and felt around under the pillow in case there were more.

There weren't.

Dissatisfied, I tucked the card into my backpack. I walked to the patio doors.

Behind the glass, the moon was nearly full. Fat and orange, it hung above the trees. Halloween was coming, and for the first time, that knowledge was unsettling.

A dark shadow moved across the lawn toward the house, and I tensed. It scuttled across a beam of light cascading from a downstairs window. A striped tail lashed, a dark mask flashing a defiant look.

My shoulders loosened. *A raccoon.*

I swallowed. Time to stop starting at shadows. It was too early for bed. If I was going home tomorrow, I needed to take advantage of all my time here.

I emerged from my room into the red-carpeted corridor. Oil paintings hung from the wood-paneled walls.

And I didn't remember that I'd promised Nick I'd stay safe in my room.

Distracted by the card, by the new environment, by Sunny's murder, I hadn't been paying attention to the end of the conversation.

I took my time as I walked toward the stairs to study the paintings. I didn't expect to find any clues in them. But they were originals, and they were good. Some modern, some old, they all had the look of being painted by an artist who knew his business and had put his (or her) soul into the work.

I smiled at a portrait of a dog posing beside a dead pheasant. The artist had perfectly captured the dog's self-satisfied expression. Glancing toward the far-off stairs, I frowned. I didn't remember the hall being this long.

I continued on. The hall seemed to stretch. I stopped short, my stomach tumbling. *Seemed to?* The corridor *had* stretched. The top of the stairs had grown smaller with distance.

I turned, my heart hammering. The other end of the red-carpeted hallway extended. The chandeliers shrank until vanishing at a distant point.

*Impossible.* The hallway wasn't that long. This was an illusion. That was all. It had to be. The dog with his pheasant grinned at me, and I started.

"You were..." I'd already walked past that painting. *Well* past it. But the dog was here, as if I hadn't moved at all.

"I was what?" Bob asked, and I jumped.

The stairs spiraled beneath me. I gasped, teetering on the top step.

Bob grasped my elbow and steadied me. Straightening, I looked wildly past the big man.

The hallway snapped back to its normal proportions with a sickening lurch. A woman in a fifties-style blue dress frowned from a nearby portrait.

He released me. "You okay? You look a little pale."

I pressed my hand to my chest. "You, ah, startled me." Had he noticed the spell? Or had I been the only one trapped in the illusion?

"Sorry." He studied the painting. "He knew his fur."

*Fur?* "What?" I massaged the spider bite.

"The artist." He jerked his head toward the painting and scratched his reddish beard. "A master at painting fur and feathers."

"Oh." If Bob hadn't experienced anything weird, then the spell had been cast on me and not on the hallway. And that meant someone suspected me. Or they *really* hated the idea of tomorrow's magical journaling session.

I swallowed. "What do you paint?"

"Spiritualist post-modern impressionism."

My eyes narrowed. There was another possibility. Bob might have cast the spell himself. Then he wouldn't have been affected by it. "I'm not familiar with that style," I said evenly.

"I may have invented the form," Bob said. "Or as a writer, would you call it a genre?" He lifted a brow.

My fingers twitched. His comment had been innocuous. So why did I feel he was mocking me? I raised my chin. "I'd love to see your work."

He studied me from beneath his bushy reddish brows. Then he turned and descended the red-carpeted stairs.

Taking that as an invitation, I followed him to a conservatory lush with plants. He led me to a windowed corner where an easel had been set up beside a table filled with paints and brushes. Canvases leaned against a wall of windows. He turned one canvas around and set it on the easel.

It was as if someone had taken a Monet and fractured it. The play of light the impressionists were known for was there. But the colors burst from the painting in a bewildering blur.

"Step back," he said.

I did as he'd commanded, and the light folded together, creating a strange coherence. I slipped my hands into the pockets of my slacks. "It's... beautiful and unsettling."

One corner of Bob's mouth quirked upward the way Nick's did, and a pang twinged in my chest. "I'll take beautiful and unsettling," he said.

"What, ah, does it represent?"

"The merging of the mundane and the spirit world, what my spirits see when they're with me. They try to show me..." Bob's hand moved, as if he held a brush, then dropped to his side.

"So you do talk to the spirits."

"I can't avoid them. They're always with me, crowding me, whispering... We can't escape the past."

I glanced at him sidelong, uneasy. Were they here with us now? "How did you meet Mrs. Winsome?"

"At a gallery show. Georgette asked me if I had a patron, and I laughed at her. This isn't Renaissance Florence. But she was sincere. What I didn't realize at the time was she's always sincere, and that attracts both good and bad people to her. She wanted to support my work, and I..." His broad face spasmed. "I let her."

He faced me squarely. "But I'm not journaling for you."

I shrugged. "It's up to you. I'm a writer, and *I* hate journaling," I admitted.

He barked a laugh. "Figures."

I sucked in my cheeks. Journaling *was* a valid form of reflection. "In fairness, I write all day. Scribing my thoughts in a journal just seems superfluous. Occasionally, when I'm digging into something important, I'll jot down notes. But the people I've coached say the journaling is helpful."

The lie pinched my chest. I hadn't coached anyone, and I hated lying. It had taken me a long time to understand that lies were spells of dark magic, and the person most damaged was the caster.

"How do you work with your clients?" he asked.

"By asking questions about recurring thoughts and emotions that occupy their minds on a regular basis. By encouraging them to be vulnerable and open, to express self-doubts and limiting beliefs that may hold them back. That's the beginning, at least."

Bob folded his muscular arms and turned to study the canvas. "Anger."

"What?" I drew my hands from my pockets.

"I'm angry at the new normal." His sunburnt face darkened. "I'm angry at people who don't care about doing the best they can for themselves and for others. I'm angry at the whining, at the demands, and then I wonder if

*I'm* the one whining and demanding. I'm angry that Sunny's dead. It was so stupid!" His chest heaved.

A dull, gray cloud settled in my chest. Georgette was right. Bob *had* had a crush on Sunny. "What exactly happened?" I asked quietly. "Do you know?"

He shook his head. "I found Berkeley pulling her from the pool, soaking wet."

I shook my head. Well, of course she'd be... *Hold on*. I scratched my cheek. "Berkeley was wet too?"

"He must have jumped in after her. I would have. There was blood..." He gulped and briefly closed his eyes.

"In the water?" Slick tiles, a slip and fall. It happened all the time. But not *this* time.

"On the edge of the tiles," he said, "where she'd hit her head. Killed by a dumbass slip and fall."

*Maybe*. "She sent me an odd email before I came," I said. "It sounded like she was under some stress."

Bob whirled on me. "She didn't kill herself." His chest heaved. His fists clenched.

Alarmed, I took a step backward. "No, of course not. I just thought she might have had a conflict with someone here."

"No. Everyone loved Sunny."

But someone hadn't. Someone had killed her.

# Chapter 4

The pool was beautiful, elegant. And the thought of swimming in it sent a shudder through my bones that had nothing to do with Sunny's death there.

The moon had gone into hiding. The black bottomed pool reflected an eerie nothing through the iron fence. I walked through its high gates. The pool lights flashed on, illuminating its stone-tile edges.

There was no police tape around the perimeter. My chest hardened. Of course there wasn't. The powers-that-be believed Sunny's death had been an accident.

Head down, I circumnavigated the pool. If there'd been a blood stain where Sunny had struck her head, it was gone now, washed away by Georgette's uber-efficient staff. But there were other sorts of evidence beyond the physical.

Backing from the edge, I relaxed my gaze. The night scene blurred, and I blinked. Shaking myself, I relaxed my gaze again. All I saw was the usual fuzziness one does when one loses focus. And that was... wrong.

A woman had died here, suddenly and violently. That would have left a psychic mark. Unless...

My face tightened. Maybe her death *had* been an accident? Had it happened so quickly, Sunny hadn't known she was dying? It was a comforting thought, something I wanted to believe. But I couldn't.

I let my inner vision drift, lowering my lids to slits, going deeper. And this time, I felt a tug in my solar plexus.

Focusing on that sensation, I opened my eyes. I allowed the tug to draw me toward the pool house, a modern Greek revival, complete with white columns.

At its door, I hesitated, then turned the ornate knob. It was unlocked.

I pushed open the door. The interior was modern, a sand-colored space with lounge chairs and an open kitchen. A door beyond led, I assumed, to a bathroom and changing area.

But I stood frozen at the threshold, unable to take another step. Bile flooded my throat. I grasped the doorframe for balance.

A spell had been cast here. A dark one. Sunny had been attacked here, in the pool house.

Swallowing, I relaxed my gaze. A dark mass of energy hung just in front of me, blocking the entry. If I'd had any doubts before, they were gone now. Black magic was involved in Sunny's death.

Nauseated, I forced myself to focus on that darkness. Its heaviness was beginning to dissipate. A thin, black line extended from it, connecting the spell to its caster. The thread flowed through the door—

Through *me*. I yelped, leaping backward, loathe to maintain any sort of contact. I stumbled against an implacable male body.

"Hey," Berkeley grasped my upper arms. Gently, he removed me from his polished black loafer. Georgette's nephew might be slender, but he was strong. He whisked a hand through his blond hair. "Sorry. I didn't mean to startle you."

I could hardly tell him he hadn't. It had been that thread, connecting the spell to its caster. I pressed my hand to my chest and automatically swiped downward, in a quick, cleansing motion.

I'd been tracking the spell. I'd *let* the spell pull me closer, so there'd always been a connection between me and it. But seeing that cord running into my chest... Revulsion rippled my flesh.

His green eyes narrowed. "What are you doing here?"

"I'm not sure," I said honestly. "Wandering. What are *you* doing here?"

"I saw you from the house." He motioned toward the stone mansion. "I was curious."

"About the journaling exercise?" I asked brightly. *Ha*.

"No. Though yes, I am curious about that too," he said, surprising me. He looked around the pool area. "The patio's slippery. You shouldn't be out here alone. Not after..." His Adam's apple bobbed. "Not after what happened."

"You sound like you think your aunt may actually be at fault." He hadn't sounded that way at all. I was lying again. But I wanted to push him.

And it worked. His jaw tightened. "No. But Georgette doesn't need more trouble."

"Is that what Sunny's death has been? Trouble?"

Berkeley turned and walked toward the black pool. He stopped beside a wooden lounge chair and studied Mt. Shasta, its peak covered in snow. "It's hurt her. You don't know my aunt. You can't tell. But Sunny's death was a blow. She..."

He turned to me. His smile was bitter. "I think my aunt always wanted to be someone like Sunny. Free."

"Georgette's not free now?"

"Money provides a lot of freedom. The ability to travel, to buy what you want, do what you want."

*The ability to whip up an UnTarot card in short order?* My breath quickened. Had she asked Bob to create it for her? He was an artist, even if he sneered at digital collage.

"But there are responsibilities too," Berkeley continued, "and she feels them. Just managing this damn estate. It's too much for one person."

"Is that why she's supporting Bob and Matt? She feels responsible?"

"Supporting." His smile twisted. "Is that what they told you?"

"Bob said she'd offered to be his patron, and he'd accepted."

His nostrils flared. "She did more than that. They're both in her will."

*Her will?* That... seemed excessive. "It's not uncommon for people to leave small bequests," I said uncertainly.

In my past life, I'd been an estate attorney. I was very glad now to have that off my shoulders. Keeping my family safe was all the responsibility I wanted.

"Small?" He shook his head. "Georgette doesn't do anything small. They'll be set for life. And they're taking full advantage."

"And you're trying to protect her?"

Berkeley laughed shortly. "I'm not sure I can. Georgette does what she wants. Come on. Let's get your journaling exercise over with."

Since I couldn't escape gracefully, I let him lead me into the mansion. I found pen and paper and led him through the first series of questions. I discovered he had a lot of negative self-talk, but I didn't learn anything about Sunny's death.

The exercise took over an hour. When we finished, Georgette appeared, demanding I join her for dessert wine.

We stayed up late into the night talking about my family, Doyle, word witchery, and Sunny. And when I finally stumbled into my guest room, I realized she'd learned more about me than I her.

# Chapter 5

I dropped onto the canopy bed hard enough to ripple the pink and green velvet curtains. On my phone, I studied Sunny's email. She'd seen the sigil for the black lodge—or at least *a* sigil. And she'd seen a cord attached to Georgette.

I picked up the Lighthouse card. Georgette *had* to have been the one who created it.

But why? To scare me? I wasn't scared, though the card *had* been unnerving. She must have known one card wouldn't result in a full-on freakout.

My scalp prickled, and I stilled. Slowly, I raised my head. There was something in the room that didn't belong.

I grabbed the bed pillows and tossed them to the floor. Another unfamiliar card lay on the smooth sheet. Pulse speeding, I cursed. Someone had been in my room.

Rising, I hurried to the tall patio windows and rattled the handles. *Locked.* My reflection in the black glass was distorted and pale. I turned hastily away.

"Two cards aren't going to panic me either," I muttered, but that was a lie too. I was rattled.

Returning to the card on the bed, I relaxed my gaze. That same faint gold and pink aura glowed at the card's edges.

So this card was harmless as well. I took a photo where it lay and texted it to my sisters. Then I picked it up and studied it. *Distraction*. I made a face. At least this card wasn't as gloomy as the last.

In fact, it was kind of... Maybe I shouldn't have had that wine tonight.

But why would Georgette leave *this* here? I rubbed the spider bite on my hand. What was she trying to say? Was it a taunt? Was she letting me know I was being distracted?

I shook my head. That gold and pink halo around the card though... It wasn't the mark of a black lodge. Quite the opposite.

My phone rang, and I answered without checking caller ID. I already had a good idea who was on the other end.

"Seriously?" Jayce asked. "Another?"

"It's not ours, is it?" I reclined on one elbow, my eyes on the glass patio doors.

"No, the card's not ours," my sister said explosively. "Where'd you find it?"

"Under my pillow. Again."

"Was your door locked?"

"I can't lock it when I'm not in the room," I said, the words rushed. I wasn't happy about the door situation either.

Jayce swore. At length. She was more proficient at it than me. But she didn't have to worry about letting an f-bomb slip around children. "Is it black lodge?" she asked.

"I can't tell for sure. But the energy is... wrong."

"But what's it *mean?*"

I tossed the card to the rumpled pink and green coverlet. "That I'm letting myself be distracted, obviously."

"Are you?" she asked.

"I am one-hundred percent focused on figuring out who killed Sunny. I found a spell in the pool house."

"Is that where she died?"

"Something happened to her there," I said. "I don't know if she was killed, or just knocked out before being dumped in the pool to drown."

She swore again. "You need to come home. Someone knows what you're doing."

"I don't think so." I shook my head. "I mean... maybe. But this card... It feels *good*." I toed off my tennis shoes, and they thumped to the wood floor.

"That could be part of its spell," Jayce said. "The most dangerous spells are the most seductive."

I raised my brows. "A spell warning that I'm being distracted?"

"Which you say you aren't. Lies are dark spells too. Come home, and we'll figure this out."

"No," I said sharply, sitting up.

"No?"

I released a slow exhalation. Jayce's suggestion was reasonable. So why was I reluctant to leave the mansion? "I need to do this. If Sunny was right, you know what's at stake."

"The lodge can't get back into Doyle. There's no way they can get past its, uh, helping spirit."

"But my family lives in Angels Camp," I said hotly, and my face heated with shame. *Stop reacting*.

"You could move," she said in a low voice.

"I'm not letting them force us into hiding. I'm not letting them—" Snapping my jaw shut, I breathed heavily through my nose. "I'm sick of being pursued. I'm sick of being scared. I'm a witch. They should be scared of *me*."

She laughed. "Oh boy."

My chest burned. I hadn't been trying to be funny. "It's not just about our safety, don't you see? Yes, we've protected Doyle. But what about everyone else? Just because we're okay, does that mean we can turn our backs on the other people they're hurting?"

"You can't even be sure it's our lodge—not *ours*, I mean, the Brotherhood—you know what I mean. You can't be sure it's *them*."

"Maybe not, but what does the Brotherhood want? What are their ultimate goals? We don't really know, do we? Maybe we *should* know."

There was a long pause on the other end of the line. "You're right. I thought starting up the mystery school would... I don't know, be our way of putting more light into the world. But it's not enough. Not if they're killing our students."

My throat closed, my free hand fisting in the bed's soft coverlet. "You don't think..." Could that be why Sunny had died? Because if so, then we'd done this. We'd exposed Sunny to danger.

I forced the thought away. If it was true... I blinked rapidly. "If they killed Sunny to strike at us, our other students may be in danger."

"We'll warn the others. But Sunny *had* detected black lodge activity. It's more likely they killed her to keep their secret, not because of... us. She knew something or found something out. So who are your suspects?" Jayce asked, brisk.

"Georgette, of course. It's her mansion. She's got the financial resources to be a prime candidate for a black lodge." They loved the rich and famous, and for some reason—ego?—wealthy celebrities made easy prey.

"Who else?"

My shoulders loosened. It was a relief to talk suspects, to move away from the idea that Sunny had died because of us. But the thought hovered in the background, an anguished ghost.

"There are three other people who were here when Sunny died," I said. "Georgette's nephew, Berkeley, and two artists she's supporting. A musician named Matt Power, and an artist named Bob Wodge."

"And their work has a supernatural bent."

"You know them?" I asked, surprised, and shifted on the bed. A floral throw pillow whumped softly to the floor.

"Just because I prefer an evening at a country bar to an afternoon in a museum, doesn't mean I am completely ignorant of modern culture."

I snorted an unwilling laugh. "Okay. Berkeley claims he's hanging around to protect Georgette from the grasping ambitions of the two artists. The fact is, she's got resources, and through her, so do all of those men."

"And at least three of them have a known interest in magic—Georgette, Matt Power, and Bob Wodge."

I nodded. Georgette, because she'd hired Sunny and through her, me. And it was no accident the two artists she patronized were inspired by supernatural themes.

"But we can't discount Berkeley," I said. "Just because we don't know about his magical life, doesn't mean he doesn't have one."

"Your magical journaling thing hasn't unearthed that yet?" Jayce asked.

"My so-called coaching hasn't exactly been an investigative win. Bob refuses to participate—"

"Suspicious."

"Is it?" I hadn't been kidding when I'd said *I* disliked journaling. "I haven't had a chance yet with Georgette and Matt. And all I got from Berkeley is that the angry voice in his head belongs to his dead mother."

"Ouch."

"He's going to work on being more mindful about it. I gave him some strategies."

"So at least you're doing *some* good." She laughed shortly.

"Oh, stop it. I'm going to bed." I disconnected and flopped onto the bed. The UnTarot card whispered to the floor.

I stared at the pink and green canopy for a minute or so. Then I got up, retrieved the card, and locked the bedroom door.

And then I shoved a chair under the ornate knob.

DISTRACTION

# Chapter 6

I sipped my coffee in the breakfast room. But I couldn't taste it.

I stared through the picture window. Had Sunny sat here, drinking coffee, taking in the same scene? The morning dew glistening on the expanse of manicured lawn. The fiery blur of trees, snowcapped Mt. Shasta rising above them in the distance. The ley lines, their energy humming.

My fingers tightened on the mug. Mt. Shasta had to be the reason these ley lines held so much power. The volcano was a cauldron of unpredictable energy.

And that was just one of the reasons I'd be gone before Halloween tomorrow. Halloween—or Samhain to us witches—was a between time, when the veil was thin. And with all that earth energy converging here, at the mansion, and a full moon...

I rubbed the back of my neck. None of that mattered. I'd leave today, well before all that magical energy converged.

A "witch yoga" instructor arrived at ten. I joined her session because Georgette insisted, and because I needed to work out. And being a witch myself, I was curious. And ultimately disappointed.

Through the poses, the witch kept up a continuous stream of chatter. True, it was witchy chatter about connecting with our ancestors as the veil thinned, blah, blah, blah.

But I didn't want to think about the thinning veil. And all the talk was distracting.

It was also impossible to interrogate Georgette while in downward dog or corpse pose. And when the class ended, before I could ask anything useful, she hurried off to a board meeting for her foundation.

Frustrated, I wandered the mansion. When I wasn't checking my watch, I searched for dark magic. I banged my thighs and shins on more than one piece of furniture in the process—a hazard of seeing with the inner rather than outer eyes.

In the massive, white-tile kitchen, I found Matt making a ham sandwich at a central island. Copper pots hung above the musician's dark head.

He paused, sandwich gripped in his long, expressive hands. "What are you doing here?" he asked.

"Same thing you are." I grabbed a slice of sourdough and started assembling my own lunch.

His coffee eyes narrowed. "You weren't looking for me?"

"Should I have been?"

"Georgette wants me to try your journaling exercise."

"And you don't?" I couldn't force him. But it might be a way to learn more about the man—and maybe about Sunny's murder.

He sighed. "Georgette has been good to me. If she thinks it will help unlock my creativity, I'll try it."

Another semi-willing participant? The men really *did* take their obligations to Georgette seriously. "It sounds like she's been influential on you. That's actually one of my journaling prompts."

"Oh?"

"To identify key individuals in your life who've had an impact on your self-perception, people like Georgette. To delve into what emotions and lessons the relationships hold."

I slapped a second slice of sourdough bread on top of my creation to hide my awkwardness. It sounded like psychobabble when I said it out loud.

"Gratitude." Matt lowered his head to study the long, wooden island. "I feel gratitude. Georgette's one of those people of light. She's helped me believe in myself, to trust in my muse. It's a gift she has."

It wasn't how one usually described a dark magician. I glanced toward the massive gas stove and frowned. "Tell me about that."

"She sees things in people that others don't, that they may not see in themselves. And she helps bring out those gifts."

"Did she do that for Sunny?" I asked.

Matt met my gaze. His brown eyes were steady and serious. "She must have. Sunny was devoted to her until—" He looked toward the windows, high in the white, subway-tile wall.

"Until she died?"

"No." Matt set down his sandwich. "I keep thinking about Sunny, about the night before she died. Sunny was so... unlike herself."

"How?"

"Tense. Normally, she was... well, she was sunny, lowercase. That night, she seemed on edge, like a darkness had fallen on her."

"And then she had her accident," I murmured.

His dark brows drew closer. "Was it?"

"You don't think it was *suicide*?" I asked innocently.

Matt's narrow face twisted in a sneer. "Of course not. You don't commit suicide by banging the back of your head on the edge of a pool."

"But you said she wasn't like herself."

"But not suicidal. She seemed agitated. Even angry."

I shot a glance at him. Earlier, he'd said *tense*. Which was it? "At whom?"

"At... She seemed frustrated with Georgette for some reason."

*Georgette again*. My chest hardened. "Why do you think that?"

"The things Sunny said. The way she moved. Normally, Sunny moved so fluidly, like a lioness. Her movements that night were jerky, uneven. It was like she was... being conducted by an amateur."

I sat back, startled. *Conducted?* Could a dark magician have caused Sunny to lose her balance at the pool? Were her uneven movements the beginnings of a spell?

But the spell I'd felt had been inside the pool house. And Sunny hadn't been in the pool house until the next morning. Unless...

"Did Sunny go swimming that day?" I asked. "The day before she died, I mean?"

He frowned. "No. That was strange too. She usually swam every morning."

"How can you be sure?"

His smile was faint. "I'm an early riser. My bedroom overlooks the path to the pool. I usually saw her going to and fro in the morning."

"The path?" I asked sharply. "Not the pool itself?" I'd think about him watching Sunny later. His spying could be innocent, or it could represent an unhealthy obsession.

"No. If I had..." Matt shook his head. "Maybe I could have done something."

"Did you see anyone else going out to the pool the morning she died?"

His eyes narrowed. "Anyone else? No. Only Bob. And he didn't kill her."

"I never suggested he had."

"Didn't you?" He pushed away from the table. Grabbing what was left of his sandwich, he strode from the kitchen.

I took a thoughtful bite of mine. It needed more mustard.

❧ ·•◆•· ☙

Georgette didn't return to the mansion until after three. The afternoon had grown cold, the color of the maples fading. I watched her 1960s Mercedes cruise to a halt on the gravel drive, and I tried to tamp down my impatience.

I'd done journaling exercises with the gardener, a cook, and a cleaning lady.

*Describe a recent event that triggered strong emotions within you.*

The discovery of Sunny's body. (Duh).

*Write about a significant relationship in your life. What emotions and lessons does this relationship hold?*

All with their families, off-site, and not involved in Sunny's death.

*Explore a secret you've held onto. How might the alchemical concept of distillation relate to the process of revealing or concealing this secret?*

The cook had been offered a job at higher pay by a neighbor. The gardener hated the new Japanese maples Georgette had insisted on planting. And the housekeeper was carrying on an affair with the gardener.

None had been at the house when Sunny had died. None had anything bad to say about Georgette. But I was having a harder and harder time buying into the philanthropist's saintly image.

"Karin! There you are." Georgette strode across the flagstones toward me, the wide sleeves of her kimono flapping. One caught on the end of the patio railing, jerking her to a stop. She muttered a curse and untangled herself. "I've been looking all over for you."

"Same here," I said.

She blinked. "You were? Why?"

"For our journaling session."

"But that's why I was looking for *you*." Her smile was wan. "Let's go inside, shall we? I'd like to journal about Sunny."

*Yes, please.* "Of course."

I followed her into a private study. Massive amethyst geodes stood in each corner. Quartz crystals lined the top of a roll-top desk. Weak afternoon light flowed through the high, stained glass windows behind the desk. The tall windows were gorgeous, in an art nouveau design, and I wondered what view they hid.

She motioned me into a floral-patterned wingchair beside a crackling fireplace. "I do love a fire, don't you?"

"They're cozy," I agreed. "There's something soothing about the sound and smell and sight."

"Exactly." Georgette sat in the matching chair on the other side of the end table. She leaned on one arm and shifted closer to me. "Now, tell me how you're getting on."

"Your staff seemed to find the journaling exercises useful."

She made a face. "But not Bob and Matt?"

"Nor Berkeley," I admitted.

"Oh, I knew *he* wouldn't play ball. The boy hasn't an ounce of imagination. He's too rigid." Her face clouded. "I worry about him sometimes."

But he had played ball, if reluctantly. "Why do you say that?"

"His rigidity, of course. People need to learn how to bend," Georgette said complacently.

In my chair, my arms tightened against my body. "Bend to whom?" *To her?*

"To life," she said. "We think we're in control, but we're not. We're only in control of our own tiny empire of one, and even then our demons are sometimes running the show." She studied the fire. "For some more than others."

"Do you think Sunny had demons?" Unlike the men, at least Georgette spoke freely to me. So freely, I couldn't quite trust what she said.

Her head whipped toward me. "Of course. We all do. But Sunny knew better than most how to keep hers in line."

I raised a brow. "I wouldn't mind knowing the secret to that."

"By loving them of course, because our demons are a part of us, even if they are embarrassing and irritating and frequently misbehave. We can't manage our dark sides by pretending they don't exist or by hating ourselves. Hate just weakens us and gives the dark more power."

Bemused, I sat back in the soft chair. It wasn't the philosophy of a dark magician. In fact, what she'd said wasn't far off from what our mystery school taught.

"Did Sunny show you the book that went along with her UnTarot deck?" I asked.

"No, she said it was proprietary. Why?"

"I guess I'm curious about what happened to Sunny's things."

She pressed a hand to her mouth and lurched from her chair. "Good lord. I completely... I don't know. They must still be in her room. I need to make sure her foster brother gets them. She would want that."

I leaned forward. "I can help pack them up, if you like." Maybe Sunny had left a clue behind.

"No, no," she said absently and walked to the stained glass windows. Curves of colored light tinted her face. "One of the staff will do it." She turned to face me. Deep lines carved the space between her snowy brows. "Or maybe it would be better if I did."

"Are you afraid they won't take care with them?" I asked. The staff I'd met had seemed refreshingly competent.

"No, I'm afraid—" Georgette gnawed her bottom lip. She drew herself up. "I'm afraid—"

Her stomach pulled inward, her shoulders angling forward in a rolling motion. She jerked backward. Her feet lifted off the carpet, her eyes widening, her kimono billowing about her small form.

Georgette reached wildly forward, as if grasping the air for purchase. The glass crashed, splintering, and she flew through the window.

# Chapter 7

I did not leap instantly and heroically into action. I'm ashamed to say I stood gaping for a too-long moment, cold blading my core. Then I shouted and scrambled through the window. Colorful shards tinkled to the paving stones around me.

Georgette lay still, blood darkening the remains of her shredded kimono. A cream-colored, jagged fragment stuck upright from her thigh like a broken gravestone.

I had to stop myself from pulling the piece free. The glass itself was putting pressure on the wound. Removing it might cause the older woman to bleed out. But there was already so much blood, blood, blood staining her jeans.

Hands shaking, I made a stuttering call to 9-1-1. The dispatcher told me what I already knew—don't remove the glass in her thigh—and that emergency services were on their way.

But how long would it take them to get here? The mansion was remote, down narrow, twisting roads. And the nearest town was small and under-resourced.

Georgette whimpered. Unthinking, I grasped her bony hand.

My insides churned. I *had* to have been imagining her skin was growing cold. It was too soon for that. But what if it wasn't? What if my witch senses were detecting death?

The fall, the lacerations... I rocked on my knees, the muscles jumping beneath my skin. Georgette wasn't a young woman.

Her colorful kimono was bloodied and shredded. A gash in her t-shirt exposed her rounded flesh. The flagstones were cold and hard against my knees. I imagined that cold seeping into Georgette's frail form.

And I began to sew.

I'm a knot witch. Threads are my business, knitting things together. My husband often joked that no one had been better than me at tying people into legal knots.

Slowly, the cuts on her arms and face healed. But there were too many, and there were more I couldn't see. I was too slow. She was going to die.

My gaze darted around the patio. Where was everyone? Surely someone would have heard the crash? "Help," I screamed.

*Don't die. Don't die.* Why hadn't I protected her?

*Sew, sew, sew.* A cut near her wrist sealed.

Sunny had tried to warn me Georgette might be in danger. But I'd misinterpreted her email and thought Georgette was the villain. I'd left my hostess open to attack. Suddenly, I found it hard to breathe.

Ambient light from the ley lines gleamed on the paving stones. *The ley lines.* They were power, magical power that could be tapped to charge spells.

A weary hiss of air escaped Georgette's mouth, and my heart clenched. She was dying. My magic wasn't strong or fast enough. It needed more power. Mentally, I reached for the lines.

My bones and muscles locked in place. My breath seized in my lungs. Energy rippled from my feet to my scalp.

I've never been one of those kids who grabbed an electric fence to see what would happen. So I don't have much basis for comparison. But if an electric fence had been charged with a lightning strike, I imagine that's what grabbing that ley line felt like.

I wanted to scream, but even that was impossible. White blinded the backs of my eyelids. I couldn't feel Georgette's hand in mine, because I couldn't tell where my skin ended and hers began.

And then it was over. My muscles released, and I was falling, muscles useless, drawing frantic gasps of air. The sky was blue and flat, and I didn't understand what it was, or that I was on my back.

I don't know how long it took for the short circuits in my brain to mend. Rolling to my side, I reached for Georgette and stopped, one hand extended. The shard of glass in her thigh was gone.

A cold weight filled my chest. *Oh, no.* What had I done? If my spell had removed the shard...

I scrambled toward her, slicing my own hand on a piece of broken glass. Swearing, I widened the rip in her jeans and examined the wound. The skin was closed, the injury marked only by a thin white scar.

I covered my mouth with one hand. Was she... completely healed?

Dizzy, I yanked up one sleeve of her kimono. Her arms were marked by smaller white lines. Though her eyes remained closed, her chest rose and fell steadily.

"Georgette," I said. "Do you hear me?"

She didn't respond. Her breathing seemed to deepen though, grow steadier. I gripped her hand and prayed.

By the time the paramedics arrived, Georgette had regained consciousness. Since the only open wound was my hand and Georgette's clothing was soaked in blood, the paramedics convinced themselves I was the source. I wanted to argue, but it was the simplest explanation outside of magic.

So I let them give me a more thorough examination than I liked. I declined a ride to the hospital though.

Georgette did too, though the paramedics thought she might have a concussion. Then they decided she'd had a mini stroke and thrown herself through the window in the process. She needed tests, scans.

But Georgette refused to leave her home, and Georgette got what Georgette wanted. Eventually, her nephew escorted her to her room.

Shaking their heads, the paramedics left. I tottered to my guest room and changed my clothing.

I studied my ruined slacks and blouse. My mouth twisted in disgust. I dropped my clothing into the waste basket beneath the antique desk. It would take magic to get all that blood out, and that was a power neither I nor my sisters had.

There was a knock at my bedroom door. I opened it.

Expression grim, Berkeley stood in the hallway. "She wants to see you."

"She's better?" I asked.

He snorted. "Nothing gets my aunt down for long."

Hoping that was true, I followed Berkeley to a massive bedroom. Where the walls weren't covered in modern art, they were covered in shelves lined with more books.

Georgette rested, her eyes closed, in a worn velvet recliner. She opened her eyes and raised her white head. "I did *not* have a stroke."

"No," I said. "I don't think you did either."

"Then what *did* happen?"

"I don't know," I lied. "I was turning to leave when I heard a crash. Then you were outside, and the window was broken."

Her eyes flashed. "Well, I didn't do it on purpose. I loved that window." Her face paled, and she leaned her head against the chair. "And I know you didn't push me through."

"How?" Berkeley folded his arms.

"I just know," Georgette snapped. She turned her face toward me, her expression softening. "You held my hand. I could *hear* you. I'm so tired. Will you stay with me?"

"Of course."

Berkeley made an exasperated noise. Shaking his head, he strode from the oversized room.

"Sit." She motioned to a nearby chair. Its cushion was decorated in delicate needlepoint, I guessed from the 19th century.

I perched on it gingerly.

"You'll tell me what really happened later," she said and closed her eyes.

I doubted I would, and my shoulders hunched. It had been attempted murder by magic.

How could I have been so wrong?

# Chapter 8

While Georgette slept, I wove a ward of magical protection around her book-lined bedroom. I considered trying to tie it to the ley lines, but the shock I'd received earlier made me think better of the plan.

The old spider bite in my palm had been blazing with pain ever since that jolt from the ley lines. But the burning sensation was a small price to pay. I just hoped it didn't signal any long-term damage.

When I finished the spell, I stepped away from her windows. The afternoon sun lowered behind the snow-capped mountain.

My ward wouldn't stop a physical attack from a normie. But it would stop a dark magician from entering the room. It would keep any black magic from it as well.

I tiptoed from Georgette's bedroom and returned to my own room, where I cast the same spell. From there, I moved on to her private study. A bitter breeze flowed through the broken window, and I pulled my shawl tighter.

Relaxing my gaze, I studied the area around the window. A dark knot of energy hovered in front of the Georgette-sized hole in the colored glass. I frowned.

Normally a spell would leave connecting energies leading back to its caster. But there was none here. And though the spell, dark and cold and greasy, was clearly the work of someone with mal-intent, there was something else in it too.

Wary, I reached toward it with my awareness. Energy crackled through me, singeing my nerves.

Rubbing the old bite, I stepped backward, my jaw tight. *The ley lines.* The magician had used them to power his spell.

The spider bite turned clammy. When I was a child, a tree had knocked down a power line. One of our neighbors had gone to move it from the street using the end of a broom. He hadn't realized the ground around the line had been energized, and he'd gotten electrocuted.

My aunt had hurried me away from the awful sight. But I could still smell his singed hair and clothing, still hear his groans of pain. I couldn't imagine trying to tap into that much energy willingly.

Two workmen appeared outside the window. They began to sweep the patio, their brooms making *hush-hush* sounds on the paving stones.

Ignoring them, I relaxed deeper, closing my eyes entirely and seeing with my third eye. The energy of the ley lines filled the room. I couldn't see the lines themselves—they were elsewhere in the house. But the corona of their powerful energy flooded the mansion in an electric fog.

No wonder I couldn't see any connecting energy between the spell and the magician. It was camouflaged in the nimbus of ley energy.

But the spell cast in the pool house had been far enough outside their convergence point for me to differentiate its cords. If I moved quickly, I might find a clue to its caster.

Hurrying outside, I jogged to the pool house. But I was too late. The energy from the spell I'd seen inside earlier had faded. All that remained was an uneasy, electrical prickling that raised the hair on my arms.

But I couldn't see the actual spell, couldn't trace it. I swore.

My phone rang in my pocket, and I pulled it free. My heart surged. *Nick.*

"Nick," I said. "There's been an attack on Georgette."

"Mommy," Emmie said, breathless, "Mit took my doll."

"Oh no," I said, scanning the pool house. There wasn't much in it. A sand-colored lounge area beside a matching open kitchen.

But if Sunny *had* been attacked here, could there be a physical trace? The police might not have searched here. "Why did he take your doll?" I asked my daughter.

"He took Miss Molly, and I can't find her, and and, he took her. And he said..." She rambled on.

I studied the smooth throw rug, then I flipped it over. There wasn't even a fluff of lint beneath it. I moved toward the kitchen, Emmie's voice rising and falling in my ear. "Is your father there?" I asked.

Prowling the kitchen, I half listened to her response. How had she learned to call me? Had Nick dialed and given her the phone?

I hoped Mitch wasn't in the process of destroying her doll. That was unlikely though. He hadn't reached the destructive-boy phase yet.

A hook of magical energy tugged at my solar plexus. I turned, letting it draw me toward a corner of the tiled counter.

Squatting, I studied a faint, brownish stain on the gray tile. *Blood.*

Sunny had struck her head here, and someone had cleaned up. But not one of Georgette's uber-efficient staff members. They wouldn't have been so careless.

I snapped a photo of the smear with my phone, then returned it to my ear. "Put your daddy on the phone, Emmie."

My daughter hung up. Childish crisis resolved?

Shrugging, I pocketed the phone. Nick would no doubt tell me when we next spoke. I returned inside the mansion, intent on finding Sunny's room. If Georgette hadn't removed her things, maybe Sunny had left a clue behind.

Berkeley intercepted me in the high-ceilinged foyer. He scowled. "Georgette's been calling for you."

I glanced up the stairs. Sunny's room had probably been along the same hall as my guest room. "I expect she wants to do her journaling exercise."

Her nephew rolled his eyes. "Not even falling through a window will stop her." He trailed me to her room and hesitated in the long hallway. "I guess I'll leave you two your privacy."

I forced a smile. *Go away.* "It's probably a good idea." I knocked gently on the door.

"Come in," she called.

Stuck, I walked inside. "How are you feeling?"

Georgette sat up in the faded velvet wingchair where I'd left her. "Annoyed." Primly, she closed the paperback in her lap. "I still can't figure out how I fell through a window. Bob insists it happened, but I don't remember a thing. You and I were talking, and then I was flat on my back with all those handsome paramedics around me. It wasn't a bad way to wake up. Was it my kimono? I'm constantly catching the sleeves on things."

Over her jeans and tee she was wearing another kimono—a blue print. But I noticed its sleeves were narrower, with pink, fur-lined cuffs.

"I don't know," I lied, worried. Physically, she seemed okay, but her memory must be rattled. We'd had this conversation before. "I'd turned to leave when it happened."

Her mouth puckered in dissatisfaction. "Well. Maybe your journaling exercise will help me remember."

I sat in the needlepoint chair near hers. "I'm not sure that would help. I prepped questions about Sunny, and the original focus of my exercise was to dig into the sources of any negative self-talk. Do you even have any?"

Georgette's smile was faint. "Oh yes. We all have demons. I've been fighting mine for..." She turned her head and looked out the window, overlooking the lawn. "My mother was an angry woman married to an angry man. In fairness, she was raised in a house of neglect and he in abuse. They were both doing their best."

She met my gaze. "I ran in the opposite direction of being quiet and accommodating."

Georgette didn't seem quiet and accommodating now. "Did that keep you safe as a child?"

She blinked. "I suppose it did. Unfortunately, I married another angry man. I suppose it felt familiar."

And patterns traveled through the generations. Absently, I rubbed my chest. "We should really be writing this down."

"My head hurts." She rubbed her brow. "I want to think about it first. I'll write tomorrow. How would you prompt me? I'm ready to be coached."

"On which? Sunny or your demons?"

She lowered her head. "I thought I was ready to talk about Sunny. But I don't think I am."

"Okay." I crossed my ankles. "Demons it is. Have you got something to write with?"

In answer, she drew a notebook and pen from a drawer in the end table by her side.

"Close your eyes. Imagine gazing into an alchemical mirror that reflects your true self, desires, and shadows."

I waited while she laid her book on the nearby end table and relaxed into the faded wingchair. She could have afforded a new chair. I wondered what this one meant to her?

"What aspects of your personality do you see?" I paused while she thought, then wrote. When she looked up, I continued, "How might these facets intertwine with your past experiences and potential paths forward?"

Georgette lowered her pen. "All I see is guilt. The past haunts my present. Is that my personality?"

"A tendency to feel unwanted guilt could be."

"I'm not sure if it's unwarranted. After my husband died, I felt... free. And guilty. And time passed and I decided to enjoy my freedom, not to remarry. I couldn't trust myself not to make the same mistake. It took decades for me to realize I had a problem, that staying closed and quiet, that not revealing any of my difficult feelings, was a lie of sorts. How could anyone really know me if I didn't tell them what I felt? And it took me more years to unlearn it." She pinched her bottom lip between two fingers. "I'm still unlearning it."

She laid one hand on the book on the small table, then pulled away. "But someone once told me that it's easier to get out of your head if you're doing something that helps others. And they were right. Now I wonder if maybe that was avoidance too. Maybe I should have stayed in my head a bit more, dealt with things."

"Is that why you agreed with Sunny that I should come?"

"Yes. As usual, I had my own selfish reasons." Her smile quickly faded.

"Maybe enjoying the feeling of doing good can be selfish, but if you're aware of it..." My thoughts tumbled over each other, as I struggled for the next words.

"What?" she asked.

"It just seems that if we've... evolved to or have been given the gift of feeling good doing good, then... it's good."

"To be a point of light," she murmured, "shining in the darkness."

"A lighthouse?" I asked, startled. Was that what the card had meant? That Georgette was the Lighthouse, and she was in danger?

"I was thinking of something smaller, like a candle, but why not go big? Why not a lighthouse? Berkeley thinks it's my money that allows me to help people. But we can all be lighthouses, can't we? Encouraging others to do their best, reminding each other of what it means to be good and honest and true."

"That's..." I looked down at my lap. An ache pinched my heart, and I didn't know why.

She yawned. "Goodness. Falling through a window does take it out of you. I think I'll turn in early tonight. Let's finish the exercise tomorrow, shall we?" She closed her eyes.

I sat there for a long moment. Then I rose and left the room to find Sunny's.

Berkeley waited in the hallway, the expression on his narrow face worried. "Well?"

"Your aunt said she's going to turn in. She's tired."

"I'll see she's taken care of."

I nodded and moved down the hall. Thankfully, he didn't follow.

"What will you do?" he called after me.

"I thought I'd just wander. It's okay if I explore the house, isn't it?"

"Yeah. Sure."

I padded to the end of the hall, my footsteps soft on the thick, crimson carpet. As I turned the corner, I glanced over my shoulder. He stood outside her door and watched me.

Giving him a jaunty wave, I continued on past the rows of paintings. And then I relaxed my gaze.

I was starting to get a better idea why a black lodge member would haunt Georgette's house. The ley lines.

But *did* the three intersect? Or did they simply come close to converging? I suspected the former. The amount of power generated was too great. But I wanted to be sure.

I found a glowing ley line, cutting across the hall and vanishing into... Gently, I rapped on the door. When no one answered, I opened it. Another bedroom, fit for a country squire.

I moved inside, but there were no bags on the floor or women's clothing in the closets or antique dresser. I made a low, disappointed noise in my throat. The room hadn't been Sunny's.

I studied the ley line. It vanished into the guest room's far wall. Continuing down the carpeted hallway, I turned a corner. The line cut across this hallway and vanished into another room.

I knocked and opened the door. A bowling alley. I gaped. Georgette had a bowling alley. And no doubt a movie theater. I stepped into the room. And also a... My breath caught.

The faint edge of a second ley line converged with the first, both vanishing into the wall. But what was on the other side?

Heart thumping, I trotted into the hall. If the three converged, the power they generated would be—

The hall lurched. I pressed one hand to the wood paneled wall for balance, my stomach turning. The hall was moving, pivoting, and I dropped to my knees, closing my eyes, my stomach pitching.

When I opened them again, the world was upside down. I gasped, gouging my fingers into the soft carpet. My auburn hair hung up (down?), my clothes bagged awkwardly. I clung to the floor, which was now the ceiling.

My breath rasped, my fingers digging achingly deeper into the carpet. But it was impossible. No matter how hard I gripped, I'd fall. Black spots swam before my gaze.

I forced my breathing to slow. If it was impossible for me to cling like a bat to the ceiling, I *wasn't* upside down. I was in no danger of falling. This was another illusion.

I forced myself to let go, and I was flying. The ceiling slammed into my back. I gasped, the breath knocked from my lungs. Panicked, I grasped the nearby chandelier. Its crystals tinkled faintly.

And then the world turned again, and I was falling, screaming, crystals raining down, and the floor rushing up, and I knew this was going to hurt, and then the world went dark.

# Chapter 9

I walked through my home in Angels Camp, but it was changed. Gone were my children's finger paintings on the refrigerator door. Gone were the tumbles of toys and books in the cream-colored family room. Gone the photos of my sisters on the upright piano.

Where had they gone?

Patting my pockets, I looked for something I'd lost, but I couldn't remember what it was. It was something... Something... I climbed the carpeted stairs and pushed open the door to Emmie's room.

Gone were the pink paint and unicorns. Posters of pouting young men with guitars hung at angles on the walls.

Numb, I crossed the hall to my bedroom with Nick. It had changed too. Now instead of comfy cozy, it was sleek and modern with blue-gray walls. I hated that color trend.

A brunette, a stranger, sat on the bed and fiddled with a gold charm bracelet. She gave a low cry of exasperation. "Why can't anyone invent a clasp you can manage one-handed?"

"What are you doing here?" I asked, too shocked to yell. "Who *are* you?"

Buttoning his cuffs, Nick emerged from the master bath, and my heart compressed. Fine lines fanned at the corners of his eyes. Gray touched the temples of his deep brown hair. He bent and kissed the woman's head. "So we husbands can lend a hand."

I swayed. *Husbands?* "Nick?" I whispered. *No, no, no.*

He bent over the woman. She raised her arm, palm up. Instead of clasping her bracelet, he raised her hand higher and kissed the skin inside the wrist.

"No," I moaned. He did that to *me*.

"Sarah?" A teen boy leaned past me into the bedroom. "You mind if I borrow your car?"

*Mitch*? My knees collapsed, and I dropped to the thick carpet. *My son*. I would know him anytime, anywhere. And he was as tall and strong and handsome as I'd predicted.

My fingers dug deeper into the plush carpet. This was the future. And I wasn't in it.

"Go ahead." The woman's voice dropped. "Your sister won't need it."

Nick blanched. He looked toward a curtained window.

I forced myself to standing. Gripping my stomach, I backed against the wall. "Why won't Emmie need it?" But of course no one heard me. I was in a vision. I wasn't here.

I wasn't here.

Heavily, I stumbled from the bedroom. I didn't want to see more.

But that was a lie. I had to see more, to know. Where was my daughter? "Emmie?"

The world spun, and I stood in a room lit only by flickering candlelight. Men and women in black robes chanted in a circle around me. I stood inside a chalk pentacle.

I felt the blood drain from my face. Not a pentacle, a *pentagram*, an inverted star, a symbol of dark magic.

"I summon you, Karin Bonheim Heathcoat," a woman intoned behind me. I started and turned.

The woman held out her hand. She drew the length of a wicked-looking dagger across her palm, and I flinched. The woman drew back her hood, and I cried out.

*Emmie.* What was my daughter doing here, with these people? Using a *pentagram?*

"No!" I reached for her, but a hard cold wall blocked my hand. Jaw clenched, I pushed against the barrier. "Emmie, this is wrong."

The chanting rose. A chill wind flickered the candle flames.

I couldn't stay. I couldn't watch anymore. Turning, I raced away from her, toward a gap in the robed magicians. I slammed into something solid and fell backward with a gasp.

*The circle.* I was trapped inside like a spirit. They'd summoned... *me.*

I was dead.

*No.* I groaned.

I was dead, and I'd missed everything. I was dead, and Emmie was here, with a black lodge. *She* was a dark magician. My jaw tightened, my throat squeezing shut.

I touched my neck, and my breath caught. But if I was a ghost, I shouldn't be able to feel my throat, my jaw. According to my sister Lenore, a shamanic witch, I shouldn't feel anything. So either Lenore was wrong, or I wasn't dead.

I closed my eyes. *Okay. Not dead.* Because I didn't want to be dead. *Think.* How had I gotten here? I'd been...

Where *had* I been? Somewhere confusing. Somewhere I didn't belong.

*No.* I'd been in a house. A mansion. There'd been a chandelier. A fall...

My eyes sprang open. *A trap.* This wasn't real. My first instinct had been correct—I was stuck in a vision that wasn't my own. "This isn't real." I turned inside the pentacle. "It isn't real," I shouted.

Something rustled by my foot. An UnTarot card lay against the tip of my sneaker. I bent to pick it up and turned it over. *Distraction.*

Yes, the vision was a distraction. But it wasn't wrong either, and my body crumpled.

I'd been so excited about getting a break from my normal life, that I hadn't been present with my family. And truth be told, I hadn't been present for a long time. I'd let myself be distracted from what mattered.

Nick and Emmie and Mitch mattered. And yes, I did deserve occasional alone time and to do things for myself. But when I was with them, even on the phone, I needed to be *with* them.

They would always be my first priority. And now they were alone.

But only for now, while I... I froze, rooted to the spot. If I was trapped in a vision, what was happening in the real world? To me? To my family?

"Wake up, wake up, wake up," I screamed.

"Hey." A firm hand pressed my shoulder. "You can wake up."

My eyelids fluttered open. I lay on a bed, beneath a pink and green canopy. Sun streamed through the glass patio doors.

Bob frowned down at me. "Good. You're back."

I sat up and looked wildly around the guest bedroom. My backpack leaned against the antique desk where I'd left it. "How'd I get here? What happened?"

"You got hit by a falling chandelier." The artist straightened away from me and put an UnTarot card on the stand beside the bed. "You've been out all night."

"All night?" I asked, aghast.

"Yeah. Happy Halloween."

My pulse sped. "Why am I here? Why didn't someone take me to the hospital?" I'd been unconscious and they'd just... left me to sleep it off?

"You got lucky," Bob said. "Georgette's private doctor was here to check up on her when we found you. They decided it was best to let you recover here."

"But..." I sputtered. I'd been unconscious *all night?* I must have a concussion. How the hell could they have not taken me to the hospital?

And then the rest of his words penetrated, and my muscles turned to seawater. "Halloween?" I wasn't supposed to be here. I was supposed to be *gone* by now.

"Yep. We took turns watching you—Matt and me."

My breath quickened, my neck and shoulders tightening. *Halloween*. A day special for my kids. A day when a place like this was most dangerous, with a black lodge member on the prowl.

A day when the veil was thin, and the moon was full, and—

I threw off the bed covers and was relieved to see I was still wearing yesterday's slacks and blouse. "I've got to go."

"Okay." Bob pushed back his chair and stood. "I'll, uh, get out of your way." The big man ambled from the room. He closed the door softly behind him.

I found my phone lying on the bedside table, and I swore. Five missed calls from Nick. I called my husband.

"I'm an hour away," he said without preamble. "What happened?"

"Emmie and—?"

"Jayce is watching the kids. I called the police last night. They said they checked on you and you were okay. What's going on?"

Gooseflesh pebbled the back of my neck. The police had said I was fine? I'd been *unconscious*. Good God, were they in on it too?

"I got hit by a..." My gaze clouded. But I *hadn't* been hit by a chandelier. Or if I had, that had come later. "There's a black lodge member here. He hit me with a magical booby trap. I'm fine now, and I'm packing. I'm leaving."

"Then I'll meet you there or on the road," he said, tone grim.

*On the road.* "Nick... I'm sorry."

"For being attacked?"

"For being so excited about doing something different that I wasn't listening to your concerns." Heat warmed my eyes. "Or to Emmie or Mitch. You come first. You always come first."

He sighed. "You're first for us too, you know."

I wiped my eyes. I wasn't usually this weepy. It was likely an effect of the shock. But I meant what I'd said. "I know," I said softly, "but... I'll see you soon. I love you."

"I love you too. Be careful."

We muttered more terms of endearment, and then we disconnected, and I got busy packing. Fortunately, there wasn't much to pack. I closed my laptop and stuffed it into my backpack then looked around the spacious guest room.

The fallen UnTarot card lay on the end table where Bob had put it. Whatever was going on with those cards, there was magic involved. Jayce and Lenore would need to see them. I picked it up and glanced at its front.

It was a new card.

SACRED SPACE

# Chapter 10

*Sacred space.* Beside the canopy bed, I stilled, understanding. Of course. The answer had been there all along, so obvious I hadn't seen it. Or I'd been unwilling to see it. Seeing it meant another failure, another willful blindness.

I slipped that card into my pack as well. Forget the mystery of the new cards. I'd puzzle that out later. Right now, I was getting out of here.

And I needed to take Georgette with me. The attack on her had failed yesterday because I'd been here. There would be another attack after I left.

Wary, I emerged from my room. Once I was relatively sure the long hallways weren't going to turn upside down, I hurried to Georgette's door.

She wasn't in her bedroom. That made my heart jump uncomfortably. Her bedroom was the only room beside my own I'd warded.

I trotted down the wide staircase and went from room to room, my pace quickening. Finally, I found Georgette in her private study. Despite the glittering chandeliers, the room was sunk in gloom, plywood affixed where the window had once been.

Georgette sat in a wingchair reading a dog-eared paperback. She looked up, her reading glasses low on her nose. "How are you feeling, dear?"

"I need to go," I blurted.

She sighed and closed her book. "I'm so sorry that happened to you. I'll of course pay for any follow-up doctor visits you feel you need. That chandelier was only installed a few years ago. There's no reason it should have fallen. I've already put a call in to the installer. We will have words," she said, grim.

"It wasn't the—" I shook my head. I needed to get her out of here. Getting into the weeds about magical attacks wasn't going to speed the process. "It's Halloween. I promised my kids I'd take them trick-or-treating."

She smiled. "Of course. I should have thought... You'll be able to make it home in time?"

"Yes, it's only a couple hours. But... I think you should come with me."

Georgette barked a laugh. "I'm afraid my days of trick-or-treating are over."

"Not for candy. You're in danger."

"My doctor—"

"Sunny was murdered. The reason I came was because Sunny was worried about you. She thought there was someone in the house who wanted to hurt you, because he wanted your house, this space." I motioned around the book-lined room.

With Georgette gone—*dead*—the house would be sold. No doubt a wealthy black lodge member would be quick to bid on it. And then they'd have access to the point of power where the lines converged. It would be like having access to a magical nuclear reactor.

They'd wanted Doyle because of its magical energies. And when they'd lost their chance, they'd turned to other places of power. Or maybe they'd always been seeking such spots, spots to increase their own magical power.

And we'd been complacent. Once we'd blocked them from our little piece of Sierra paradise, we'd sat back, job done. But it hadn't been done. I remembered that vision of my daughter in the black lodge. My stomach tightened.

But it wasn't just about my family's possible future. They were still hurting other people. And magical attacks weren't the sort of thing the police could investigate or the courts could prosecute.

They were the sort of thing only witches like my sisters and me, like the other women in our mystery school, could fight. And we'd fallen down there as well. We hadn't expected them to *have* to fight, and so we hadn't prepared them, hadn't warned them.

And Sunny had died. My throat hardened.

I steeled myself, expecting objections from her, denials. But Georgette's wrinkled face whitened. She seemed to shrink, grow smaller in her chair. The paperback slipped from her fingers and hit the very expensive rug.

"This house?" she whispered.

I exhaled slowly. "You suspect someone," I said. "You know."

"I didn't—" Georgette shook her head. "Not until you said... Oh, no." Her pale eyes widened. She pressed a hand to her mouth.

"Let's get out of here," I said. "We can figure it out later, but right now, we need to go."

"I don't think so," Berkeley said from behind me.

Scalp prickling, I turned. Her nephew aimed a gun at my midsection, and ice spread through my core.

# Chapter 11

A gun. I hadn't expected anything so prosaic.

I should have.

But holding the gun on me was a smart play. Georgette, being a good person, sat still as a mannequin in her wing chair. She wouldn't make a move with me in danger. And next to Berkeley, I was the second-most dangerous person in the room.

"Matt and Bob won't be joining us," Berkeley said, breaking the tide of shocked silence. He stepped deeper into Georgette's study, his polished shoes stopping at the edge of the Persian carpet.

He wore a tailored blue suit, his dress shirt open at the collar. *Professional clothes for dirty business.* Angry heat flushed my veins. The gun, a black semiautomatic, was steady in his slender hands.

Georgette's fingers pressed deeper into the soft arms of her chair. "What have you done to them?" She leaned forward.

"They're unharmed, just... confused." One corner of his lips lifted.

My jaw tightened. I had a good idea what sort of confusion spell they were trapped in. Upside down, crawling along the ceiling, or imprisoned in an unending hallway.

I glanced toward the plywood-covered window. Not that there'd be any chance anyone would see Berkeley even without the plywood. Not on this estate.

"I haven't decided yet which one of them I'll blame for your murders," he continued. "Do you have any preferences, auntie?"

"I'd prefer you put that damned gun down," Georgette said in a low voice.

"That's not an option," he said.

"You don't have to do this," she said.

"Unfortunately, I do." He scowled, his eyes flashing. "You've left me no choice. We're running out of time. I *have* to act before the Ebon Gaia is completely destroyed."

Georgette's rounded face crinkled with confusion. "Ebon Gaia? What does that mean?"

"Ebon means dark," I said slowly, not taking my eyes from the gun.

"Ah yes." Berkeley sneered. "I forgot you're a writer too, even if it is only romances."

"You made a mistake," I said, ignoring the "only romances" comment. "You shouldn't have let them take me to my bedroom."

Berkeley hadn't been able to pass the ward I'd left there, or the ward on Georgette's bedroom. I'd never seen him go inside her room after I'd laid it.

"What I don't understand," I continued, "is how the doctor got past my ward. He's one of you, isn't he?"

"That normie? No. But he does what I tell him. I pay him well enough for that."

In her chair, Georgette made a soft, pained noise. Light from the chandeliers cast craggy shadows on her expressive face.

"And the local police?" I asked. "Do you pay them too?"

"Of course. Money is power," he said. "One form of it, at least."

"And you'll inherit Georgette's," I said, sickened.

"No," she said firmly. "He won't."

"No," he agreed. "She's tied it up in her useless art charities. But she's left me this estate, and that's all we really need."

"We?" Georgette asked, her voice thin.

"His black lodge friends," I said. "He's a member of a society of oc-cultists called the Brotherhood."

Berkeley started. I flinched, but the gun didn't go off.

"You *are* a witch," he said.

I stiffened, my skin tingling. The Brotherhood knew all about my sisters and I, but it seemed Berkeley didn't. Which meant he probably hadn't bothered to tell them that a witch or two had been nosing around his aunt's. He'd thought he could take care of us himself.

And in fairness, he'd been doing a pretty good job on that score. I swallowed. "So was Sunny. You weren't as clever as you thought. She knew there was someone from the Brotherhood on the grounds, and she told me. And you killed her."

I should have realized Berkeley was behind this sooner. The energy of that dark spell from the murder in the pool house hadn't just been flowing through me. It had been flowing to Berkeley, standing behind me at the time.

"It was unfortunate," he said, his tone urgent. "I feel terrible about it. But I caught her on my computer after I'd stepped away. She was reading my emails from the Brotherhood. She tried to play it off, but..."

"But you killed her," Georgette said quietly.

He shrugged. "Sunny resisted my first spell. It's a shame to lose someone that strong. But there are bigger things at stake. That email was *private*."

She'd resisted Berkeley's first spell? That must have been the spell Matt had clocked. The jerky movements he'd noticed had been her fighting it off.

"You're strong too," he said dismissively, "but you're too late. My power is wired into the convergence of ley lines now. I have my own aura of protection."

I relaxed my gaze. A cold, blue-black razor of light surrounded him, and my stomach plunged. A golden line flowed steadily into his protective aura.

He was feeding the power from the ley lines into his own magic, using them as a battery.

*Son of a...* He'd figured out how to tap into them without overloading like I had. And I was part terrified at that thought, part embarrassed by my failure. My nostrils flared. Berkeley would win. He had all the power.

He'd win, and I'd be dead, and then Nick would come, and Berkeley wouldn't hesitate to kill him too. Not with the police in his pocket. Nick would die, and our children would be without us both.

My mind raced. I couldn't let that happen. I couldn't let the lodge get their talons in Emmie.

Senses open, I could feel the power of his protective aura, hard and implacable. My jaw ached. I'd never be able to break through. My knot magic had never been particularly good at offense.

Lines and knots and strings and cords and cables were my business. Not...

I studied the line of power feeding his protective aura. *The line.*

"You can see it," he said. "Now you understand."

"Leave Karin out of this." Georgette's voice quavered. "She's done nothing to you."

"But she knows everything," he said. "I'm afraid she's in it, whether we like it or not."

*A power line.* I hadn't had my powers when I was young. But now, cords and cables were my business.

"But why do you want this house so badly?" Georgette asked. "I don't understand. What do you *want?*"

"Look at this waste." He motioned toward the broken window with the gun. "All this space for one woman. The environmental footprint alone is ridiculous. We'll put it to much better use."

"For what?" she asked.

"For radical human degrowth. Call it... extinction, if you like."

"Extinction?" Her forehead wrinkled. "I don't understand."

I thought *I* did, but I couldn't let his crazed ramblings distract me. Mentally, I felt along the connecting line, hoping for a point of thinness, a weak thread.

"I don't *want* to do any of this," he said. "I've been forced into this by the lack of action by governments and elites like yourself. Do you think I don't suffer? The pain and anguish that Sunny experienced is the pain that *I* feel when I think of our future if things don't change."

My nails bit into my palms. *His* suffering? Of all the narcissistic...

*Not now. Focus.*

Georgette leaned forward in her chair. "Berkeley, if you want the house, I'll *give* it to you."

"No," he said, "you won't. You'll betray me. Your kind always betrays."

Her pale blue eyes flashed with anger. "Not everyone's like you, Berkeley!"

"And there it is." He sneered. "You've always thought you were above me."

"That's not what I meant," she said.

*Dammit.* There *were* no weak points. My fists clenched, and for a second I was back in our yard, a child staring in horror at our poor, electrocuted neighbor. I smelled the polyester of his clothing, seared to his skin.

If I did this... Nausea tinged with acid fear rose in my throat.

What happened to me didn't matter. My family was what mattered. I visualized a blade of energy, sharp and wicked.

"It's because of people like you that the Ebon Gaia is dying," Berkeley said. "I have tried to do things another way. I've marched. I've gotten political. But it's only when we take direct action that anything changes. *You've* caused this. Sunny's death is your fault, not mine."

I pushed away the memory of that electrocution, of the shock I'd received yesterday. I pushed away the fear.

There was no choice. If I didn't break the line, we'd be shot, and Berkeley'd get away with it.

Oh, my sisters would fight. But the lodge would fight back. And Emmie was vulnerable, would be even more vulnerable without her parents at her side. But we *would* be around. Or at least one of us would be.

The blade hardened, taking form in my mind. I tasted something sour, and still, I hesitated. *Just cut the damn line.* Violet energy raced along my blade's edge.

"Your Ebon Gaia doesn't sound like much of a goddess if she's dying," Georgette snapped. "What sort of a goddess would ask you to murder?"

"Murder?" he raged. The gun in his hand trembled. "*You're* the murder-er. Your kind kills and destroys and ravages the Earth. We're only running a rearguard action. But the Ebon Gaia is with us," his voice rang out. "Your burning cities and starving children and fleeing refugees are only collateral damage in her war. Her justice is savage, and innocence is immaterial. Consider yourself lucky you won't be around to see the end." He straightened his arm.

I swept my blade through the power line. A jolt of pure ley energy lifted me off my feet. Electric agony fired along every nerve ending in my body. I shrieked.

I hit the floor hard, staggering into an end table and tasting blood. Berkeley gasped and stumbled.

The end of Berkeley's magical power line hit the wood floor beside his polished shoe. The burst of energy when it struck the floor raised the hair on my head. Berkeley was closer to the strike point though. The flare blasted him to the ceiling.

It was a high ceiling, with beams painted in the Alpine style. There was a loud crack—his bones or the burst of power—and then he crashed to the floor and lay still.

# Chapter 12

"But the police," Lenore said, her storm-colored eyes serious. She straightened her conical witch hat. It accentuated the pallor of her skin and white-blond hair. "You said Berkeley was paying them off. How did you get out of there, even if he *was* unconscious?"

Flickering jack-o-lanterns lit the path. Nick carried Mitch. Keeping pace with Emmie's little legs, my husband minced up the long gravel path to our neighbor's front door.

Our children were dressed like superheroes. Though Emmie had demanded a cheap costume from the store, they both looked adorable. And I wanted her to admire superheroes, even cheap dime store ones.

On the sidewalk, I focused on my two sisters. "Unfortunately for Berkeley, the nearest hospital was in the next town, covered by a sheriff's department rather than the town police. The sheriff arrested him in the hospital for the murder of Sunny and for the attempted murder of Georgette. His deputies went back to gather the evidence from Georgette's pool house."

And the stain I'd found *had* been blood. The test results weren't back yet, but I knew it was Sunny's.

"He took a crack at you too," Jayce said. She hadn't bothered with a costume, wearing jeans that hugged her curves and a tight, sapphire v-neck sweater. "Rich people get all the attention. It isn't fair."

Lenore frowned, her pale face creasing. "Poor Sunny. I feel like... we failed her, didn't we?"

"We couldn't have known." Jayce clawed a hand through her thick, mahogany hair. "And Sunny wasn't targeted because of us."

"She was targeted because of what we taught her," I said. "We taught her the signs to look for. But we need to do a better job teaching protection."

Jayce cleared her throat and looked toward the lit house. "It's, ah, sort of already happening."

*Already happening?* I loved my sister, but no one would call her proactive. "What do you mean?" I asked.

"There's a new UnTarot card," Jayce said. "It's called *Protection*. Several students contacted me this morning, asking where the email to go along with it was."

I stared, horrorstruck. *Others* were getting the new cards? I'd assumed the problem had been confined to me. "How is this happening?" I asked.

"We *did* cast that spell on the cards," Jayce said weakly, "asking for inspiration to manifest. I think Doyle gave our spell more juice than we expected."

I muttered a curse. A passing mother dressed like a zombie shot me a dark look, and my face warmed.

"There's more," Lenore said. "I reached out to some of our students. They reported that the cards and emails are coming out of order. But the students didn't *think* they were out of order. They arrived at the perfect time for the issues they were dealing with. But the emails aren't in the order we set them up."

I gaped. "Are you saying the school is... making its *own* decisions?"

Lenore shrugged. "They seem to be pretty good decisions. The cards helped you, and the magic on them *is* positive."

I rubbed my spider bite. It still burned from the shock of slicing that power line.

"No." I gave a violent shake of my head. "There's too much we don't know about this. We need to shut down the email sequence."

Lenore and Jayce exchanged glances.

"What?" I asked.

"We, um, sort of tried that." Jayce shuffled her booted feet.

"It didn't work," Lenore said.

"How can it not work? It's an email drip!" A gang of masked kids trooped past, and I lowered my voice. "We pay a monthly fee," I finished.

"Not anymore," Jayce said. "We canceled the service, but the emails are still coming."

Lenore cleared her throat. "On the plus side—"

"How can any of this have a plus side?" I asked.

"It does save us some money," she continued. "We weren't making anything on the school."

Who cared? "That's not—"

"It's strange," Jayce said. "Whatever spell or magic is doing this, it seems able to generate cards in the material world. But it can't create new email texts to go with them." She looked at me expectantly.

The lack of new email texts was the *least* strange thing about the situation. *Wait. What?*

"You want *me* to write the new emails?" I asked, indignant. Lenore was a *poet*. What was stopping *her* from penning an ode to The Lighthouse?

"You did a pretty good job interpreting the cards you received," Lenore said. "And you wrote up the text on our other cards. I think it's—he's—our ah, friend in Doyle, is expecting you to finish the job."

My eyes narrowed. "You *think?*" Doyle's *anima locus*—its spirit of the place—was big and furry and had a decidedly weird sense of humor. Which may have had something to do with the big and furry part.

But because of him (it?) Doyle was protected. Other places weren't. And our mystery school now had a mind of its own.

Lenore's skin pinked. "I journeyed on the question. So, no. I don't *think*. We talked. I know."

"What else did our *friend* say?" I asked.

"Nothing," Lenore said. "He's not very, er, verbal."

A bat wheeled above us, a tiny black silhouette against Sierra stars. They were spotlight bright. Even when in darkness, our Sierra home was spectacular. And we could have lost it to a black lodge, if we hadn't gotten lucky.

We had been lucky. Sunny had not been.

Throat tightening, I studied my tennis shoes. "It's not enough," I said in a low voice. "We have to track what the Brotherhood is doing. We may have protected Doyle, but there are other sacred sites, other ley lines, and other witches who might encounter the lodge." *Witches like Emmie.* "Whether they're students or not, we can't let them come up against the Brotherhood alone."

"I agree," Jayce said, surprising me. "At the end, when we were in trouble, we had help. We founded the Mystery School so we could give other witches the training we didn't have, so they wouldn't make the mistakes we made."

She swallowed and was quiet for a long moment. Children shrieked "*Trick-or-treat!*"

"This is important," Jayce finished, her voice uneven.

Emmie raced up to me, her eyes bright behind her red mask. "Mit didn't say thank you."

"He didn't?" I knelt to get on eye level with my daughter. "Well, your brother's still learning. That's why it's important for you to set a good example, to be... a lighthouse. Did *you* say thank you?"

"Yes."

I hugged her. "Good girl." And we'd discuss the complicated ethics of snitching later.

Nick ambled up to us, his chiseled face relaxed, his dark hair sleek. Grasping a mini candy bar, Mitch leaned from his arms and held it out to me. His black superhero cape bagged where Mitch held him.

"Is that for me?" I asked, taking the candy from his hand.

Mitch buried his head in Nick's broad chest. "He's a little tired," Nick said.

I rubbed my son's back. "It's been a big night."

"I'm glad you're here for it," Nick said, his gray-blue eyes intent.

"I'll never miss an important family event," I said. "Or phone call."

Nick bent and kissed me. "That wasn't meant as a criticism."

"I know. But I've allowed myself to get distracted from what matters. And I don't want to do that anymore."

He smiled. "Then let's go home."

Seeker:

As you progress along the path, you'll be tempted to urge others to improve their own situation. This is generally a positive instinct, but it needs to be handled with care, ensuring it's coming from a place of love rather than ego. Please contemplate the next card in your deck.

**The Lighthouse**

*Being a light for others. Letting your light shine.*

It's easy to get frustrated by the actions of others and tossed by the storms of life. Ultimately, we can't force others to change their course. We can't force the world to be what we want it to be. But we can be a lighthouse and show them the way (whether they follow the light is up to them). We can be a model, let our own light shine, and be the best people we can be.

This card asks how we're showing up in life. Are we leading by example? Are we giving the people in our life the light and support they need?

The symbols:

A lighthouse stands high on a dark cliff, hidden in the fog. A storm-tossed ocean roils beneath. Glimmers of moonlight appear in the clouds.

The questions:

Who in your life is struggling? How can you shine for yourself and for others?

***

**Author's Note**

Though this is the "last" book in the Doyle Witch series (or is it?), Karin will be back in the start to my new spin-off series, The Mystery School, which starts with book 1, *LEGACY OF THE WITCH*. And if you buy it direct from the author HERE, you can get some exclusive extras!

You can also get the UnTarot app for free! Just click the link to https:// untarot.beezer.com and save it to your favorites on your laptop or phone. If you allow notifications, you will get weekly Mystery School Mindsets—inspirational action items from the school—plus updates about upcoming paranormal mysteries by Kirsten Weiss. (You can also add the icon to your phone's homescreen, but I've been having issues with this and being a mystery writer and not an app designer, am baffled as to why. If you do download it, please let me know how it works for you).

You can use the UnTarot for divination, self-reflection, and journaling. The UnTarot deck not only serves as a portal into the unknown but also aligns with the world of the Mystery School series. Unveil the mysteries, embrace the unknown, and prepare for an experience that transcends the boundaries of fiction and reality. Step into the world of the UnTarot, where every card tells a story, and every story reveals a secret.

Follow Kirsten Weiss on social media and subscribe to her newsletter for the latest updates on the upcoming Kickstarter campaign and the first full-length novel in the Mystery School series, *Legacy of the Witch!*

***

**If you enjoyed this book, please tell your friends about it!**
**Click to share on Twitter!**
**Click to share on Facebook!**
**Or here's a sample post to copy and paste:**

*I just got done reading HARVEST OF THE WITCH and I loved it! If you're a fan of Amanda Lee, Kim Richardson, and Tricia O'Malley, I recommend checking this book out. https://bit.ly/HarvestWitch*

# Legacy of the Witch

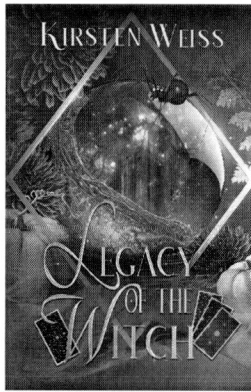

*S**eeker: As societies grow increasingly fragmented, hopelessness, nihilism, and division are on the rise. But there is another way—a way of mystery and magic, of wholeness and transformation. Do you dare take the first step? Our path is not for the faint-hearted, but for seekers of ancient truths.*

All April wants is to start over after her husband's sudden death. She's conjuring a new path—finally getting her degree and planning her new business in bucolic Pennsylvania Dutch country. Joining an online mystery school seems like harmless fun.

But when a murdered man leaves her a cryptic message, she catches glimpses of another reality she's unwilling to acknowledge. A reality where bygone enchantments cast cryptic shadows, and the present brims with unanswered questions.

As April works to unearth the mystery, every step brings her closer to a truth she's been evading. And to a conspiracy of hexes that may end in her demise.

Legacy of the Witch is a spellbinding, interactive tale of a woman's midlife quest to understand the complexities of her own heart. A paranormal women's fiction murder mystery for anyone who's wondered if there might be more to their own life than meets the eye...

**Book 1 in the new Mystery School Series, featuring the UnTarot deck. Start reading now!**

**Turn the page for a sneak peek of *Legacy of the Witch!***

# Sneak Peek of Legacy of the Witch!

O f all the life-ruining mistakes I'd ever made, being late was not going to be one of them.

I double checked the campus map. My advisor's office *should* have been directly ahead of me. Instead, there was a wide swathe of grass dotted with crimson leaves and way-too-young students.

At least they seemed too young to *me*. They had to be too young, because the alternative was that at forty-seven, I was too old. Too old to start over. Too old to rid myself of my growing collection of ghosts. Too old to get a degree. Too old to use that degree as a springboard for my dream business and dream life and dream whatever the hell I was doing.

But I couldn't think that way. I had to have hope or I'd be stuck in the purgatory of widowhood.

I crumpled the campus map in my gloved hand. What *was* I doing? Everything was shifting—inside and out, above and below, and—

"You lost?" A man who could have been in his twenties grinned, attempting a covert up and down glance. At least I still warranted the occasional masculine appraisal.

"I'm trying to find the Heritage Building," I said. And I hated being late. My usual timeliness came from the Penn German in me, though I'd never lived in Pennsylvania before now.

He pulled a phone from the rear pocket of his ripped jeans, tapped the screen. The man nodded past a maple, its remaining leaves splashes of fire. "It's thataway."

I grimaced. "Thanks." *Duh.* I could have used my phone to find the building. But I'd grown up on paper, not screens. "You're a lifesaver." Stomach churning, I trotted across the damp lawn.

"Any time," he called after me, and I gave him a wave without looking back.

I'd only been on campus a few days in the last year—quick flights in and out. Most of my folk art program was online. Until now. Today would be my first in-person meeting with my thesis advisor.

Ghosts of disappointments trailing behind me, I jogged across the pavement to the three-story brick building dotted with cupolas and white-painted eaves. I pushed open a door and hurried inside the high-ceilinged foyer, its pointed arches adorned with elaborate wood carvings.

The campus wasn't as grand as the bigger colleges and far from Ivy League. But Babylon College was up and coming. More importantly, it had the degree I wanted in the area I wanted to be.

Though it hadn't come cheap, it didn't come with an Ivy League price tag either. Still, at the thought of the expense, guilt tangled with my anxiety, and suddenly, I found it hard to breathe. The life insurance had been there to get my life back on track after—

"It was supposed to be an investment," my husband whispered. "A safety net."

My throat tightened. I shook my head, trying to dislodge the echo of Jordan's voice. The past was past, and this was present, and present wasn't the time for ghosts. If I didn't focus, I'd be late for my future.

*Office 302. Third floor.* I glanced at a cluster of students waiting outside an elevator. Jogging past them, I climbed the wide, wooden stairs.

I huffed down a hallway, my low heels click-clacking on the linoleum. How late *was* I? I skidded to a halt in front of room 302. A brass nameplate glittered on the door:

DR. EZEKIAL STOLTZFUS.

The air molecules in the hallway compressed, my ghosts squeezing closer. My father, skeptical. My mother, curious. My husband, sardonic. Not for the first time, I wished I could see rather than just sense them. If I could see them, I'd know they were real.

Forcing myself to breathe, I reached for the door.

It opened before I could touch the knob. An auburn-haired woman in a navy jacket looked back over her shoulder. "Nonetheless, if you think of anything—" She plowed into me, and we stumbled apart.

"Whoops," she said and laughed. "Sorry. You okay?" She was a little shorter than me—maybe five-seven. Her hair was darker than my true, pale red. And of course she was younger, somewhere in her late thirties. A professor? Another not-too-young student?

"No harm done." I straightened the front of my forest-green blazer.

A man with thick, dark hair streaked with gold loomed over her shoulder. "April?" he asked. He wore a navy suit with faint, gold pinstripes, his white shirt open at the collar.

I nodded, and he broke into a grin. He had a lovely, even smile, the outside corners of his brown sugar eyes crinkling, and my stupid heart jumped. "You're right on time," he said. "Come in."

The woman sidled past me.

I was definitely *not* right on time, but I wasn't going to argue the point. "Thanks for seeing me, Dr. Stoltzfus." I walked into the office.

"We're too old for titles. Call me Zeke."

My mouth pinched. I wasn't *that* old, and my advisor couldn't be over fifty. But *Zeke* was less of a mouthful than *Stoltzfus*.

He shut the door behind us and motioned toward a cluttered wooden desk. "Have a seat."

Bookshelves lined the walls. Spider plants lounged on a windowsill overlooking the lawn I'd just raced across. Behind the glass, students scurried, heads bent, across the thick grass.

I pulled back a rolling chair and sat, tugging off my gloves.

My advisor walked around his desk and dropped into the executive chair opposite. He gusted a breath and motioned toward the closed door. "Sorry about that. It was another of those witches."

I blinked. *Ah, what?* Had the college's folklore program expanded to witchcraft? "Witches?"

He pulled a tie from the pocket of his suit jacket and dropped it beside a stack of papers marked in angry red ink. "You'll come across a share of them in your research. *Braucherei* is hot in the witchcraft world these days. American witches are looking for western magic so they can't be accused of cultural appropriation."

My gaze clouded. "You mean... powwow?" It was old Pennsylvania Dutch faith healing. Silly stuff, superstition. I was surprised the practice still existed.

"There's some controversy over that name," he said. "Not that the Penn Dutch care. They're in their own world. But the pagan community and the academics do."

I glanced back toward the closed door. "And she was a witch?" I asked, twisting the gloves in my lap.

"Has her own online mystery school, if you can believe it," he said cheerfully. "But let's talk about your thesis proposal." His brown eyes grew serious, and his chin lowered. "Tell me the truth. Why are you *really* studying Pennsylvania Dutch folk art?"

I froze in my chair. *Dammit.* He knew. How did he learn about my plans? I'd only told a few friends, and they were far from Pennsylvania. I cleared my throat.

"Why?" I repeated stupidly.

"Yes," he said patiently and flashed that Hollywood smile again. "Why?"

I hesitated. I couldn't tell him the truth, that I wanted to start a business selling modernized versions of Penn Dutch décor. He'd think I wasn't serious about my masters.

Though I hadn't been a student long, I already knew the drill. *Real* researchers were doing the research for its own sake, not for crass commercial purposes. Women like me, women who wanted a degree to bolster their credentials after decades with no work history, were unserious.

I pasted on a smile in return. "My parents were Penn Dutch. They moved to California before I was born, but we spoke Penn Dutch in the home—"

"Right, I remember reading that you spoke it. That's a real advantage in this work. Aside from me, there aren't many people on campus who speak the language."

"It's been super useful," I said dryly, and he chuckled. Only 300,000 people spoke the language, a High German mashup. Penn Dutch was a dying tongue. At the thought, an ache pinched my chest. There wasn't much I could do about it, but I hated to see the old culture vanish.

I cleared my throat. "Anyway," I continued, "I love painting—"

"Most folk artists do."

I shifted in my chair, its wheels squeaking on the linoleum. *Artist.* The word sounded pretentious—at least when applied to me. "I think of myself more as a craftsperson. Anyway, I fell in love with the primitive style, with the folk art, but I wanted to make it my own."

"The mark of a true artist."

My face warmed. *Flattery will get you everywhere.* "But I realized if I was going to make it my own, I needed to first master the original forms. Which is why I'm getting this degree."

It wasn't a lie. I *did* want to know more, to be better. There was always so much to learn.

"Those are all good reasons," Zeke said. "Maybe that explains your proposal."

The office darkened, a cloud passing before the sun. In the window, the spider plant's green stripes seemed to fade.

I glanced down at the gloves in my lap. "What do you mean?" I'd thought my proposal explained itself. After all, it was a *proposal*.

"What you're proposing to research is old ground, I'm afraid. You're going to need to find something new."

*Oh come on.* I mustered a smile. "But... it's folk art. It's history. It's *all* old ground."

"Then find a new angle on it. Maybe look at how other local artists are re-interpreting the folk art."

My stomach plunged. I didn't want to study modern artists. I didn't want their work to influence mine. Worse, what if a technique or idea lodged in my subconscious, and later I came to believe it was mine?

Zeke cocked his head. "Actually, that witch may have done you a favor. Apparently, someone's been putting up odd hex signs in the woods." He chuckled. "It's causing a minor panic. It's probably just a prank, but who knows? Why don't you look into it? It's folk art. It's new. It's interesting."

I relaxed. *Hex signs.* I hadn't planned on selling them, since they mainly went on barns and my shop would focus on interior decor. Hex signs could work. "I'll look into it."

"Not that you have to do hex signs," my advisor said quickly. "It's just a suggestion."

"No, no," I said. "It's a good one. I'll check it out." Though I was a little annoyed I'd have to. I'd liked my old proposal.

"Unfortunately," Zeke said, "the only hex sign manufacturer, Zook, went out of business during COVID. But there's a local farmer who's painting hex signs in the modern style. You might want to chat with him..." He scrolled through his phone. "Here's his contact info. What's your cell number?"

I recited it to him. A moment later, a contact pinged into my texts.

"There you go." He rose. "I hear you got one of the king's cottages?'

"The what?"

His smile broadened. "Mr. King, our local philanthropist. I heard you got a scholarship to stay in one of his cottages. I hope you got one close to campus."

"Not exactly. I'm up in Mt. Gretel." It was about a thirty-minute drive—reasonable given the low rent.

"Oh." His voice lowered as he drew out the word. "They stuck you in the haunted forest."

*Haunted*? I shifted in my chair, and my gloves whispered to the linoleum floor. I bent to retrieve them. "The what—?"

He lifted a well-manicured hand. "No, it's not really haunted. It just seems that way off-season. Mt. Gretel's lovely, if a little lonely this time of year."

Far off or not, I was lucky I'd got the cottage. Mr. King had made them available to only a few grad students. And the woods were gorgeous in October, when the leaves were turning.

We said our goodbyes, and I made my way back to my Honda. *Hex signs.*

The colorful round signs actually had nothing to do with hexes or witchcraft. A guy who'd written tourist books in the 1920s had gotten confused, saying the signs were used to ward off curses and bad luck. Later, enterprising folk artists had realized that the supernatural sells and had run with the idea.

Scowling, I pulled onto the highway. *New ground.* Why did it always have to be *new ground* in academia? Why couldn't I just prove I knew my stuff and move on?

The highway narrowed, gold and crimson and tangerine branches blocking out the weak sunlight as I rose higher into the hills. My Honda crested a ridge, and the highway sloped downward.

My grip loosened on the wheel, and I rolled my head. A few droplets of rain splattered my windshield.

I stopped at a supermarket for supplies then continued on to Mt. Gretel. *Haunted*. I snorted. If the tourists were too dumb to come to Mt. Gretel in the fall, that was their problem. The resort village was gorgeous any time of year.

I drove past 19th century Gothic Revival and Queen Anne cottages. Thick fall foliage partially hid the homes' faded pastels. Slowing, I passed in front of an old yellow meeting house and turned onto a narrow road.

I spotted the squat driveway to my temporary home, Cornflower Cottage. Painted a soft blue, the cottage was built into the hillside, with parking at the mid-level. Beside the porch steps was the stack of fallen branches I'd cleaned up after yesterday's storm.

I'd have to figure out what to do with them. They were too wet for firewood.

I stepped into the cheerful entryway, my hobbit-door keychain swinging in the lock. Extracting it, I kicked off my shoes, and walked toward the open kitchen with my paper bags.

Something brushed against my ankle, and I yelped, lurching away at the touch. A black cat hopped onto the wooden dining table in front of the stone fireplace. Unblinking, she gazed at me, her eyes golden.

My pulse steadied, and I laughed unevenly. "Who do you belong to?" I set my bags on the nearby kitchen counter. The room was open plan, the high, gray granite counter dividing the kitchen from the front entry and dining area.

The cat yawned, displaying razor teeth. It was an appropriate response to an inane question.

"Well, you don't belong to me." I moved to pick her up. The cat deftly evaded my grasp, hopped from the table to the rag rug, and scampered out the open door.

I shrugged. The cat probably belonged to a neighbor. Though she hadn't worn a collar, she had looked too sleek to be a stray.

"Okay then." I closed the door behind her and unloaded the bags, filling the modern fridge.

Though Cornflower Cottage was historic, it had a modern kitchen and baths. I climbed the stairs, careful to duck before I hit my head on the low overhang. Some wag had taped a handwritten reminder on it that simply read:

OUCH.

The second to highest step groaned theatrically at my weight. I walked down the narrow hall to my cramped bedroom. Its floors bowed, angling downward toward the four walls.

I dropped onto the bed, and the mattress squeaked a protest. *A cat.* I flexed my foot. Maybe a cat was what I needed.

I hadn't had a pet since I'd married Jordan. He'd said we moved around too much to be fair to an animal, and he'd been right. He was always right. It had been about as annoying as you'd expect.

I switched from professional clothes to jogging gear. I'd followed Jordan on his jobs across Europe and Asia. Wherever we'd gone, there'd been two consistencies in our lives: *The Lord of the Rings*, and my jogging.

Alas, a shared love of Tolkien had not been a solid foundation for a marriage, and Jordan had hated exercise. He'd claimed it wore the body out sooner. I hated running too, but I'd kept it up to be contrary. *Stop thinking about Jordan.*

I locked the cottage when I left, though there seemed little point. My advisor, Zeke, had been right. The village was mostly deserted, the windows dark in the cottages I passed. *Haunted.* The oaks shivered in a sudden gust, their dying leaves fluttering to the pressed stone.

I consulted my trail map, then folded it into my jacket pocket. Jogging down the leafy road, I cut down another lined with pines and found my way to the King Railway Trail.

According to the tourist brochures, my patron, Mr. W. King, had been the driving force behind turning a disused railway track into a hiking trail.

The track was now gone, replaced by a pavement and pressed stone trail that ran from Babylon to Mt. Gretel.

I liked the idea of the trail. I liked the hopefulness behind it, of taking something disused and turning it into something new and beautiful and loved.

At the trailhead, grasping branches arched above the sign. Curtains of spiderwebs hung from the bushes and rippled eerily. Insects—prey—hummed in the thick bracken. Resolutely, I pulled my thoughts from Tolkien's dark forest and its giant spiders, and I checked the map again.

START HERE ➤

Jamming the map into the side pocket of my thick leggings, I started off. My running shoes drummed a heavy beat on the pressed stone dotted with damp, yellow leaves.

*Jordan, Jordan, Jordan.* My heart heavied. He didn't like how I was spending his life insurance money. Though his opinion now shouldn't matter. Jordan was gone. And though he'd never really approved of my interests, somehow, it still *did* matter.

Through the oaks, I could occasionally catch a glimpse of a distant cottage. A shudder of droplets plopped from sodden leaves to the ground. I glanced between the snare of branches at the mercury sky and hoped any serious rain would hold off.

I didn't pass anyone. The trail was as deserted as the village, and the muscles between my shoulders loosened. I put on more speed, driving out thoughts of the past, the future, my thesis, my imaginary business.

A creek chattered, invisible, in the woods. It could have been ten feet away or a hundred. It was impossible to tell from my vantage on the trail.

I rounded a bend. A low ring of stone, about ten feet in diameter, stood beside the trail. I slowed, curious. The circular structure was too big to be an old well.

Panting, I walked toward it. The stone ring had a pagan feel, reminiscent of ancient stone barrows. Something bright and yellow and slick peeked from the undergrowth inside the ring.

I propped my foot on the stone ledge, bent to stretch my hamstring, and gasped. My hands turned clammy.

A rain slicker. It was a rain slicker.

And there was someone inside the yellow coat. A silver-haired man.

For a moment I thought it was a bad joke, he wasn't real. Then, heart banging, I hopped over the stone ledge.

Heedless of the brambles tugging at my clothes, of the muck squelching beneath my shoes, I stumbled to the supine man. He lay staring with one broad hand pressed to his chest. Blood stained his neck and pooled in the hollows around him.

"Oh my God," I breathed, fumbling for the phone in my jacket pocket.

His head turned toward me, and I yelped.

I dropped to my knees beside him. "You're alive. It's okay. I'm calling for help now." What had happened to him? Had he tripped and fallen? But what had he been doing in the circle?

"Can you put pressure on the wound?" I asked. If he couldn't, I'd need to. I'd need a cloth, something to staunch the flow.

*But first, help.* Hands shaking, I called 9-1-1.

He lifted a hand and pointed toward the trees. "Look beneath," he whispered. "The brotherhood."

"It's okay," I said. "I'm calling now." I pressed the phone to my ear. "I'm calling..." My voice faded.

His blue eyes grew as cold and impersonal as the Atlantic, and he stared without seeing at the sky. A thick dullness fogged my chest. I was too late. He was dead.

Continue the adventure with *Legacy of the Witch!* Click here to get it on Kindle!

# More Kirsten Weiss

**The Perfectly Proper Paranormal Museum Mysteries**

When highflying Maddie Kosloski is railroaded into managing her small-town's paranormal museum, she tells herself it's only temporary... until a corpse in the museum embroils her in murders past and present.

If you love quirky characters and cats with attitude, you'll love this laugh-out-loud cozy mystery series with a light paranormal twist. It's perfect for fans of Jana DeLeon, Laura Childs, and Juliet Blackwell. Start with book 1, *The Perfectly Proper Paranormal Museum*, and experience these charming wine-country whodunits today.

**The Tea & Tarot Cozy Mysteries**

Welcome to Beanblossom's Tea and Tarot, where each and every cozy mystery brews up hilarious trouble.

Abigail Beanblossom's dream of owning a tearoom is about to come true. She's got the lease, the start-up funds, and the recipes. But Abigail's out of a tearoom and into hot water when her realtor turns out to be a conman... and then turns up dead.

Take a whimsical journey with Abigail and her partner Hyperion through the seaside town of San Borromeo (patron saint of heartburn sufferers). And be sure to check out the easy tearoom recipes in the back of each book! Start the adventure with book 1, *Steeped in Murder.*

**The Wits' End Cozy Mysteries**

Cozy mysteries that are out of this world...

Running the best little UFO-themed B&B in the Sierras takes organization, breakfasting chops, and a talent for turning up trouble.

The truth is out there... Way out there in these hilarious whodunits. Start the series and beam up book 1, *At Wits' End*, today!

## Pie Town Cozy Mysteries

When Val followed her fiancé to coastal San Nicholas, she had ambitions of starting a new life and a pie shop. One broken engagement later, at least her dream of opening a pie shop has come true.... Until one of her regulars keels over at the counter.

Welcome to Pie Town, where Val and pie-crust specialist Charlene are baking up hilarious trouble. Start this laugh-out-loud cozy mystery series with book 1, *The Quiche and the Dead.*

## A Big Murder Mystery Series

*Small Town. Big Murder.*

The number one secret to my success as a bodyguard? Staying under the radar. But when a wildly public disaster blew up my career and reputation, it turned my perfect, solitary life upside down.

I thought my tiny hometown of Nowhere would be the ideal out-of-the-way refuge to wait out the media storm.

It wasn't.

My little brother had moved into a treehouse. The obscure mountain town had decided to attract tourists with the world's largest collection of big things... Yes, Nowhere now has the world's largest pizza cutter. And lawn flamingo. And ball of yarn...

And then I stumbled over a dead body.

All the evidence points to my brother being the bad guy. I may have been out of his life for a while—okay, five years—but I know he's no killer. Can I clear my brother before he becomes Nowhere's next Big Fatality?

A fast-paced and funny cozy mystery series, start with Big Shot.

## The Doyle Witch Mysteries

In a mountain town where magic lies hidden in its foundations and forests, three witchy sisters must master their powers and shatter a curse before it destroys them and the home they love.

This thrilling witch mystery series is perfect for fans of Annabel Chase, Adele Abbot, and Amanda Lee. If you love stories rich with packed with magic, mystery, and murder, you'll love the Witches of Doyle. Follow the magic with the Doyle Witch trilogy, starting with book 1, *Bound*.

### The Riga Hayworth Paranormal Mysteries

Her gargoyle's got an attitude.

Her magic's on the blink.

Alchemy might be the cure... if Riga can survive long enough to puzzle out its mysteries.

All Riga wants is to solve her own personal mystery—how to rebuild her magical life. But her new talent for unearthing murder keeps getting in the way...

If you're looking for a magical page-turner with a complicated, 40-something heroine, read the paranormal mystery series that fans of Patricia Briggs and Ilona Andrews call AMAZING! Start your next adventure with book 1, *The Alchemical Detective*.

### Sensibility Grey Steampunk Suspense

California Territory, 1848.

Steam-powered technology is still in its infancy.

Gold has been discovered, emptying the village of San Francisco of its male population.

And newly arrived immigrant, Englishwoman Sensibility Grey, is alone.

The territory may hold more dangers than Sensibility can manage. Pursued by government agents and a secret society, Sensibility must decipher her father's clockwork secrets, before time runs out.

If you love over-the-top characters, twisty mysteries, and complicated heroines, you'll love the Sensibility Grey series of steampunk suspense. Start this steampunk adventure with book 1, *Steam and Sensibility*.

# Connect with Kirsten

You can download my free app here:

**https://kirstenweissbooks.beezer.com**

Or sign up for my newsletter and get a special digital prize pack for joining, including an exclusive Tea & Tarot novella, *Fortune Favors the Grave*.

**https://kirstenweiss.com**

Or maybe you'd like to chat with other whimsical mystery fans? Come join Kirsten's reader page on Facebook:

**https://www.facebook.com/kirsten.weiss**

*Or...* sign up for my read and review team on Booksprout:

https://booksprout.co/author/8142/kirsten-weiss

# About the Author

I write laugh-out-loud, page-turning mysteries for people who want to escape with real, complex, and flawed but likable characters. If there's magic in the story, it must work consistently within the world's rules and be based in history or the reality of current magical practices.

I'm best known for my cozy mystery and witch mystery novels, though I've written some steampunk mystery as well. So if you like funny, action-packed mysteries with complicated heroines, just turn the page...

Learn more, grab my **free app**, or sign up for my **newsletter** for exclusive stories and book updates. I also have a read-and-review tea via **Booksprout** and is looking for honest and thoughtful reviews! If you're interested, download the **Booksprout app**, follow me on Booksprout, and opt-in for email notifications.

BB bookbub.com/profile/kirsten-weiss

g goodreads.com/author/show/5346143.Kirsten_Weiss

f facebook.com/kirsten.weiss

instagram.com/kirstenweissauthor/

# Other misterio press books

Please check out these other great *misterio press* series:

Karma's A Bitch: Pet Psychic Mysteries

by Shannon Esposito

Multiple Motives: Kate Huntington Mysteries

by Kassandra Lamb

The Metaphysical Detective: Riga Hayworth Paranormal

Mysteries

by Kirsten Weiss

Dangerous

and Unseemly: Concordia Wells Historical Mysteries

by K.B. Owen

Murder, Honey: Carol Sabala Mysteries

by Vinnie Hansen

Payback: Unintended Consequences Romantic Suspense

by Jessica Dale

Buried in the Dark: Frankie O'Farrell Mysteries

by Shannon Esposito

To Kill A Labrador: Marcia Banks and Buddy Cozy Mysteries

by Kassandra Lamb

Lethal Assumptions: C.o.P. on the Scene Mysteries

by Kassandra Lamb

Never

Sleep: Chronicles of a Lady Detective Historical Mysteries

by K.B. Owen

Bound: Witches of Doyle Cozy Mysteries

by Kirsten Weiss

At Wits' End Doyle Cozy Mysteries

by Kirsten Weiss

Steeped In Murder: Tea and Tarot Mysteries

by Kirsten Weiss

The Perfectly Proper Paranormal Museum Mysteries

by Kirsten Weiss

Big

Shot: The Big Murder Mysteries

by Kirsten Weiss

Steam and Sensibility: Sensibility Grey Steampunk Mysteries

by Kirsten Weiss

Full

Mortality: Nikki Latrelle Mysteries

by Sasscer Hill

ChainLinked: Moccasin Cove Mysteries

by Liz Boeger

Maui Widow Waltz: Islands of Aloha Mysteries

by JoAnn Bassett

Plus even more great mysteries/thrillers in the *misterio press* bookstore

Manufactured by Amazon.ca
Acheson, AB